"I'm here. What do you have to say to me?" Her hands were folded on the table in front of her and she sat straight, her posture unbendable, her chin high. The smug woman who sat across from him intended to be confrontational. He decided to take a different approach.

"First, hello, Avery," he started and when she didn't smile at him he started to lose his patience. "All right, what lie have I told you?" Pushing back in his seat he watched as her eyes shut momentarily, opening to stare back at him with a loathing he'd never seen from her before.

"Do you get many women with your line?"

"What line, Avery?"

She rolled her eyes at him, shaking her head, her voice deepening to a mock male tone. "'I live only for the moment. I believe in love and marriage, but not for me.'" She paused and drank from her glass, adding, "'I'm sterile, so I won't foist myself on an unsuspecting woman who might change her mind and decide she wants a family. Nobody gets hurt when it ends, no false positives!'"

"No lie, Avery, I was being honest with you that night at Jack's." His mind instantly conjured up a memory of her in a red dress. His first glimpse of her had had him heated and erect.

"And how does your wife feel about your honesty?" This time she held his gaze and didn't blink. He knew she watched several emotions wash across his face, waiting to see how he'd respond.

.

The Proxy Wife

by

Cheryl A. Cornell

This is a work of fiction. Names, characters, places, and incidents either are the product of the author's imagination or are used fictitiously, and any resemblance to actual persons living or dead, business establishments, events, or locales, is entirely coincidental.

The Proxy Wife

Contact Information: info@thewildrosepress.com

Cover Art by *Angela Anderson*

The Wild Rose Press
PO Box 708
Adams Basin, NY 14410-0706
Visit us at www.thewildrosepress.com

Publishing History
First Champagne Rose Edition, 2009
Print ISBN: 1-60154-538-X

Published in the United States of America

Dedication

For Rich, My Mister Amazed

Chapter One

"You Lied To Me!"

"About what?"

The exasperated look on his face made her want to believe there was a mistake, but she knew the only mistake made was that she had trusted him. Glancing around the local grocery she frequented, Avery forced a smile toward the checkout clerk, Wanda, who watched the exchange closely. His large hand ran through the top of his dark hair, longer than when she'd seen him last.

"Please, just go away," she started and watched his brown eyes flare at her.

"Not until you tell me why you're so upset with me," he hissed, leaning close to her ear, his words measured with each breath. She knew looking at him would be her undoing so she forced herself to stare past his shoulder.

"It doesn't matter, Mitch." Her defeated tone bothered her more than it should have; at first sight she was ready to forgive him. Staring at her, he didn't try to hide his open appraisal. She wondered what differences he saw; they'd parted four months earlier. She knew from her own daily appraisal that her face was fuller, her whole figure rounded, and her eyes clearer.

"Avery, I have to leave in the morning and you haven't answered my messages. Have supper with me tonight and we can figure out what you think I lied to you about."

"There's nothing to figure out; it's all in living color for me. Blonde, to be precise."

"What?"

He didn't rein in his surprise and she stilled him with her hand on his arm, her eyes searching behind him.

"Please, Mitch, don't make a scene. This is my neighborhood."

"I know that, Avery. I called your showroom and Helen told me you were heading home for the day."

"Helen," she breathed. "I'll kill her tomorrow. She knows better," she grumbled under her breath in Italian, knowing Mitch could understand a few phrases

"She didn't give me your address, Avery; she just said you'd gone for the day. Now, are we going to talk like civilized people or am I going to make a scene in the grocery store? I'm sure the man behind the meat counter will come to your rescue..."

Glancing past him again, she nodded to Vito, his slight elderly frame still erect for his short body height. A small laugh bubbled up in her throat at the visual of the older man jumping over the counter to aid her and she didn't hold it back. She visibly relaxed before Mitch's eyes.

"That's the Avery I know. Please, whatever has happened, don't I get a chance to defend myself?"

His brown puppy dog eyes would be her downfall. Deciding how to handle him, she glanced at the items in her cart and back to him, hating the array of healthy food she'd selected, wanting ice cream and cookies instead of carrots and celery.

"I'll meet you at the coffee shop on the next corner in half an hour. That should give you plenty of time to come up with another lie." He grabbed her upper arm and held her in place when she went to move away.

She looked at his hand on her and then to his face and he released his grip. It was a look he'd seen before but hadn't been on the receiving end of. Now he knew how Mr. Kent had felt and she laughed a second time.

"Will you show up?"

His voice was tense and she realized he was not going to go away until they talked and he'd had his say. Best to get it over with and move on. "Of course, if only to get you out of my life."

Pushing the cart with renewed enthusiasm, she headed towards Wanda, knowing to confront her would be better than to fuel the stories that might be circulated. His hands moved beside hers on the cart and she refrained from pushing him away from her.

There were no formal introductions, just small talk about the weather as her purchases were rung up. Wanda blushed as she eyed the tall, dark stranger, her look leaving nothing to the imagination. Avery pulled money from her wallet only to see Wanda accept the bills Mitch handed her, both of them watching her. Her smile was forced and she lost no time in leaving the grocery behind. When they were outside in the cold February air she turned to him.

"I said the coffee shop in half an hour. Then you can justify your lies." She made no attempt to sooth the wounded look on his face and grabbed the handles of the canvas tote bag containing her purchases from his hands. There was no look back or even a glance. She walked purposefully forward toward her townhouse. The two short blocks seemed like an eternity but she focused on getting home and putting the food away.

Out of habit she stopped by the front door to check her hair and lipstick before braving the cold to meet Mitch. She knew if she gave herself time she'd find too many reasons not to meet him and if she did that, he'd show up on her doorstep. While neither was appealing at this point in time, she decided a public place was better.

She'd go and listen to him, come home and try to forget how much she'd loved him and how badly he hurt her. She rubbed her hands over her stomach and smiled. Hesitating for only a second longer, she left before she changed her mind. Confrontation now would be better. Only then could she get on with her life. She'd made her choices and it was up to her to push past this awkward point and look forward.

The heat he created within her started its ritual burn inside her, fanning her want to new levels. Avery forced herself to push it aside. "Hormones," she said aloud before stepping onto the sidewalk. Knowing Mitch as she thought she once had, she'd known she'd hear from him again. The knowledge only reinforced her possessive attitude towards her baby. She wouldn't let Mitch or anyone else intrude in their lives and she certainly wouldn't fall for any of his lines.

****

Mitch sat in a window booth of the small coffee shop she'd directed him to. In the late afternoon, the space was mostly empty. It was well past lunch time and the early supper crowd hadn't started yet. He wasn't surprised to see her enter; he knew she would come. Mainly because if she didn't she knew he'd seek her out again.

The wind all but pushed her through the door and she waved to the waitress behind the counter. There were several hand motions exchanged before she walked confidently to his table, pulling off her gloves and camel-hair coat, tossing both on the booth seat next to her. Moments later, the waitress arrived with a metal container and a tall glass with a vanilla milkshake frosting the outside. He watched as she pulled the paper from the straw and took a long drink before settling back and staring openly at him.

"I'm here. What do you have to say to me?" Her

hands were folded on the table in front of her and she sat straight, her posture unbendable, her chin high. The smug woman who sat across from him intended to be confrontational. He decided to take a different approach.

"First, hello, Avery," he started and when she didn't smile at him he started to lose his patience. "All right, what lie have I told you?" Pushing back in his seat he watched as her eyes shut momentarily, opening to stare back at him with a loathing he'd never seen from her before.

"Do you get many women with your line?"

"What line, Avery?"

She rolled her eyes at him, shaking her head, her voice deepening to a mock male tone. "'I live only for the moment. I believe in love and marriage, but not for me.'" She paused and drank from her glass, adding, "'I'm sterile, so I won't foist myself on an unsuspecting woman who might change her mind and decide she wants a family. Nobody gets hurt when it ends, no false positives!'"

"No lie, Avery, I was being honest with you that night at Jack's." His mind instantly conjured up a memory of her in a red dress. His first glimpse of her had had him heated and erect.

"And how does your wife feel about your honesty?" This time she held his gaze and didn't blink. He knew she watched several emotions wash across his face, waiting to see how he'd respond.

"I've never been married, but somehow you think I have, so let's start there. Avery, who do you think is my wife?" At least now he knew what prompted her attitude. Hope rushed through him; straightening out this mess just got easier. *Well, he knew what he was up against*, he thought to himself.

Avery let out a sigh and leaned forward across the table, her reply short and tense. "Blonde woman, about five-foot-four, short hair, blue eyes, and heavy perfume? Ring a bell? How about the woman you sent to get me off your back?"

He had to clear this up before he told her why he was in Manhattan. At the moment that would have to wait. "Sent? I never sent anyone to see you; I've been in Australia the last three months and a few weeks up at the lodge. I came here because..."

"Mitch, your wife came to see me, she returned my letters, opened, I might add, and passed along your message. I got it loud and clear."

This time his jaw dropped and he stared at her in disbelief. "I know nothing about letters and I didn't send anyone to see you, Avery. That's the truth, believe it or not." The loving reunion he'd looked forward to dissolved before him, anger taking precedence. She was still talking while he tried to digest all the information.

"How many times have you done this to her, Mitch? How may other women has Alexandra ended your relationships with for you?"

"Alexandra?" He was stunned. Alex! The picture cleared but it didn't help. The woman he loved sat across from him and believed he was a married man. And apparently Alexandra was the reason. His hands wanted to tighten into fists and he fought the urge. He'd deal with her later; right now, Avery was his first priority.

"Ah, the light dawns." She laughed at him. "Mitch, if you were a cartoon, the light bulb would have just appeared over your head!" Pouring the rest of her milkshake into her glass she took another sip. "No quick reply to that one?"

"Alexandra works for me. I've never been married to her or anyone else, damn it. And I never got your letters or sent her to see you." His voice was emphatic with his declaration; he had to make Avery believe him. He watched the sidewalk outside trying to compose his private thoughts. "What did your letters say?"

"It doesn't matter anymore. I should go," she

said.

The hurt she'd carried the last weeks went too deep to trust him immediately, at least until she knew for sure the real situation. Knowing Alex had visited her, he understood her position, even if it did make him want to spit tacks and strangle Alex. She seemed torn between staying to hear him out and leaving before he did any further damage. He reached his hand across the table towards her.

"*No*, wait, please. Avery, what did the letters say? It's important for more reasons than you know right now." Mitch never thought he'd see Avery, of all people, turn from him. His situation just worsened another level.

"I want to believe you, but it hurt too much. I won't let you destroy me or my confidence again. Thank you for your gift; let's just leave it at that."

"Gift, what gift?" She laughed at him until tears filled her eyes. She wore an oversized sweater with jeans, natural and comfortable.

"Mitch, I don't want anything from you. I know you never want to marry or deal with children. I'm financially secure thanks to the high roller commission and I'm capable of doing this on my own. In fact, any other way is unacceptable."

"Do what, Avery?" It was a stand-off.

When she finally met his look, he saw the hurt she carried, and it was due to him--or Alex, in reality. Anger flashed through him again and he knew it would do him no good until he had all the pieces of the puzzle. His anticipation and the dreamy scenarios that got him through the last few months dissolved around him. All he saw in her eyes was hate and distrust; the loving way she'd looked at him before was gone.

****

Nothing was going to be resolved and the more they pushed the uglier it would most likely get. Mitch nodded as the waitress refilled his cup and

Avery declined a fresh shake although she really wanted another. Silence stretched between them. They were both momentarily caught up in their private memories. Avery knew she had to end this; the want to reach out to him was overwhelming. If she didn't get away from him her common sense would evade her, again.

"There's a paper I'd like you to sign for me; it absolves you of all responsibility, financial and otherwise. I'd feel better with it, Mitch. This way we both know where we stand. I'll be assured you won't show up at our door some day and you'll know there'll be no call for financial help or moral support."

He'd seemed confused before; now he was curious. "Let me see the paper, maybe it will clarify this whole situation."

"I don't have it on me. Give me an address and I'll mail it to you."

"We don't seem to have any luck with me getting your correspondence." He tried to tease her and fell flat. "I'll take you to a late supper and you can give it to me then."

"No, no meals or dates, no close quarters, Mitch. I admit I can't be around you and think straight."

He stood and dropped money on the table. "Come, I'll walk you home and you can give them to me now." There was no real room in his tone to make changes and she didn't want to make a scene here either.

"All right, but you have to promise not to touch me." His eyes became huge brown saucers and she wanted to pity his feigned confusion.

"That's a difficult promise to make."

"I'm sure Alexandra wouldn't like to hear that." It was an effective way to shut down their reunion. Pulling on her coat, she waved to the waitress as they left the shop, tugging on her gloves as they walked. "There's no sense in prolonging this. I'll give you the affidavit and you'll leave, quickly and quietly, all right?"

"You'll give me the papers and after I read them we'll decide." His hand on her back helped guide her through the pedestrian traffic.

She wasn't surprised he'd been to her building earlier in the day looking for her so he knew exactly where to head. A man like Mitch Hamilton always researched his prey. And that was how she'd felt at one point, just after her meeting with his wife. There were no feigned pleasantries. Avery paused to hang her coat in the hall closet but didn't offer to take his, speaking bluntly.

"Wait here, I'll get them."

Mitch wandered into the front room and accessed the space. He tried to see if from her perspective. It was open and airy, inviting. The furniture suited the high ceiling and the Aubusson rug centered the space. She'd matched antique tables and lamps with overstuffed furniture and blended high style with comfortable contemporary. Standing before the window overlooking the street, he heard her come down the stairs and turned to look at her. There was no conversation or pleasantries; instead she foisted the envelope towards him.

"Here, take them and leave, please?"

Turning to take the offending envelope he tucked it in the inside pocket of his jacket. "I'll get back to you after I've read this." Moving past her, he hesitated, his hand reaching to touch her cheek. She stilled at his movement and closed her eyes against his touch.

"Damn it, Avery, this isn't finished." He strode from her home, pulling the door sharply closed behind him.

Mitch read and re-read the document and couldn't believe his eyes. His brain went into shock and his body followed. Somehow, Avery had decided that he'd gotten her pregnant. It was impossible. None of this made sense. He wasn't married to anyone, especially Alex, although he knew it would have been her fondest hope. And he knew he wasn't able to father a child. He'd been up front with Avery about that from the start. If she was pregnant, it surely wasn't his.

He hailed a cab and sat in the dark back seat while the driver fought with rush hour traffic. He had no idea what he'd say to her, but he knew it had to be settled, and quickly. While he'd made the stopover just to see her, he hadn't figured on this type of greeting. Hell, it was going to be hard enough to tell her what was really on his mind. Now he couldn't, not until this was all straightened out.

****

She'd known instinctively he'd come back although she figured it would be in a day or two, not two hours later. Now she was sorry she'd changed into comfortable leggings and an old, man-tailored shirt. At least it hid the growing bulk of her belly, although for how much longer she didn't know. In the last weeks her body had taken to doing strange things. Her breasts were sensitive and already bigger. Good God, she'd thought, by the time the baby's born they'll be down to my knees. Her normally slim waist had no definition left at all.

She hit the buzzer to let him in and waited at her front door, locking him in and the cold night air out. He was taking off his jacket as he entered her hallway, dropping it on the stairs, walking into her living room. Before her stood the businessman she'd known he could be but hadn't experienced. The man who loved her with his body and soul was gone.

****

His finger leaned on the bell and her voice was cold when she answered it. "Let me in, Avery." His statement was blunt and to the point.

"Avery, I need to see the letters you wrote me,

do you still have them?" He looked her over from head to toe, his eyes taking in the slight differences since he'd seen her last, since he'd held her. Without thinking, he moved towards her, his hand coming to rest flat against her stomach, warmth seeping through the material. "You really did it," he started, but was stopped with her reply.

"No, Mitch, we really did it. Did you sign the paper for me?"

The feel of his hand on her deepened his inner need and he fought to tamp it back. "I want to see the letters first." He reluctantly pulled his hand back from her body heat, his own body betraying his want as he stiffened inside his tight jeans.

It was a stalemate of piercing looks until she turned and left him alone. Several minutes later she returned and handed him a manila envelope. She left him just as quickly and disappeared down the hallway. Mitch pulled the contents from the envelope and paused to pick up the smaller pieces that littered her floor when he did so. Two letters were intact, the third in about ten pieces. Moving to the couch, he used the flat surface of her coffee table to put the pieces together like a puzzle. Then he read each one.

The oldest one was simple; I need to talk to you, it's important. The second said basically the same thing. It was the third one, the torn letter, that got his attention; "I need you to sign the enclosed document and return it to me as soon as possible." He could only assume that meant the custody release she'd handed him earlier in the day. Mitch let the weight of his head fall into his hands as the information finally jelled. Avery returned and placed a mug of hot coffee before him.

"Don't get too excited, it's decaffeinated." She sat across from him, her legs tucked up beside her on the sofa. "Are you going to sign the affidavit for me? I really don't want anything from you, Mitch. I only want you to leave me and the baby alone."

His head flew up and he caught her look. "Avery, if there is a chance that I'm the father of your baby I won't let either of you go. As for Alex, I'll deal with her later." He sipped from the mug and tried to reason with her.

"You knew when you left the lodge I was heading to Australia for three months. Alexandra works for me in Atlantic City. I transferred her to Las Vegas to give Bob a hand getting the hotel up and running smoothly. I never saw these letters or knew of their existence. Do you really believe I'd ignore you, no matter where I was in the world?" Did she really believe he'd used her and tossed her aside? No wonder she hated him.

"In the beginning I didn't want to think so. I figured you hadn't gotten the first one, but when there was no response to the second I went to see my lawyer. We discussed the possibilities and decided it would be best to let you off the hook altogether.

"Alexandra showed up here five weeks ago, claiming to be your wife. She told me you were sterile and that I was playing a cruel game with you. She insinuated that I was a fling and didn't know of your…condition. I didn't tell her any different. She left after tossing the letters at me and threatening to press charges of blackmail and extortion if I tried to contact you again." She paused then added, "She never returned the first affidavit I sent with the third letter. I gave you my copy to sign." Her hand moved to her belly without thought, as if to protect their child.

Mitch sat back heavily in his seat, not believing what he heard, yet he knew Avery wouldn't lie about it. Why would she? With all the information going through his mind the one thing that kept coming back was that there was a possibility… "Avery, please believe me, it's important. I never sent Alexandra; I never saw your letters and I still can't believe it's possible that I fathered your baby. When Jack mentioned in passing last week that he'd run into you and you were expecting, I figured you'd gone to the clinic. I made this stopover to congratulate you and…" He didn't verbalize the rest of his reasons.

"No clinic was necessary, Mitch. I trusted you. I believed you when you told me you were sterile." The cup in her hands garnered her attention.

"But we were still careful. We used protection every time we made love, you wouldn't let me near you without it," he said, more for his own sake than hers.

"Yes, except in the pool." Her eyes flashed to his and he instantly remembered being buried inside her, the warm water taking the weight of their bodies as he moved with her. A sly smile formed on his lips at the memory.

"I was at the lodge; it's not the same there without you."

She laughed outright at him and shook her head. It was the first time he'd seen her smile in almost four months.

"Avery, I'll get back to you in a few weeks. I'm heading to Scotland. When I get back, we'll talk." He stood to leave, gathering the letters and the affidavit together before putting them all back in the larger envelope. At her door, he pulled on his jacket and turned to her, watching as she leaned in the doorway.

"You don't have to get back to me, Mitch. Just sign the paper and send it back."

"If you're carrying my child, Avery, we'll get married as soon as possible. I'll be in touch."

"*No.*" Her voice carried the weight of her convictions and she stilled before continuing. "I am carrying your child and I won't marry you. The first thing you told me about yourself was that you never wanted to marry or have a family. I refuse to have my child or myself be a burden to anyone." She didn't hesitate to add, "We deserve better. I'll not settle, even for you!"

"We'll talk; I'll get back to you." He turned to leave, then changed his mind. He moved quickly towards her, quicker than she realized when she started to back away. His hands moved beside her head, trapping her against the wall within the circle of his body.

Mitch knew he was treading on thin ice with her, but couldn't help himself. His head dipped down and captured her lips under his, his hand moving to the back of her head, angling her to meet his hungry mouth, the coffee mingling on their tongues.

He wasn't punishing or forceful, rather he tasted her, renewed his memories of her and took the kiss he'd been dreaming about for four months. The tip of his tongue traced her lips and she opened for him automatically, a small groan escaped when she did. His hand still cradled her head and his other arm slid around her waist, pulling her body against his to find his waiting desire, tight and ready, eager for her to ease his need.

Her hands went to his chest but she didn't push him away. Instead, she pulled the leather of his jacket between her fingers and tugged him tighter to her. Only the hard swell of her belly was different between them; the heat and passion she ignited within him were still ever-present. His hand left her head and slipped down to rest on her hip.

"Avery, I'll be in touch, and you will marry me."

"No, I won't. Let us go, Mitch, please?"

"No. I'll get back to you." He hesitated before pulling away from her and taking out his wallet. He offered her a white card and she shook her head, not taking it from him. He laughed at her and slipped it in the pocket of her shirt. "Use the cell number if you need me in the next few days, and, Avery, you will marry me, one way or another. If it's true that I fathered your baby, we will be a family, a very happy family at that." His lips stole one more light kiss before he turned and left.

****

Her voice mail didn't surprise her nine days later when she hit the button and heard Mitchell's clear, deep voice speaking to her.

"I'll be in transit for the next two days. Please have supper with me Friday night, seven o'clock. I'll pick you up. And, Avery, unless I hear from you on the cell number I left with you, I'll expect you to be there. We have several things to discuss. I've sent along some papers for you to read and familiarize yourself with before we meet."

She pushed the disconnect button with a strange apprehension. "Just what did that mean," she said aloud, wondering what she was supposed to familiarize herself with. She had the affidavit made up, spent hours of time and thought about how it should read and what it should say. All she wanted was the signed paper back.

Avery wondered if he had himself tested and finally found out that his long-carried weight had been lifted from his shoulders? If that was the case, she'd have to be very careful to remind him that her plans were made before their time together and she was quite capable of handling this on her own. It would leave him free to finally search for the one woman he really wanted to have his children and spend his days with. A woman like Alexandra, slim and petite, eye candy for his arm. When Avery pictured Mitch with the other woman, she saw a perfect picture.

Lately she could hardly stand to imagine herself beside Mitch, as tall as him and broader than ever before. With the baby on board, her self-image was taking a severe hit. And she knew it would only get worse before "little bit" finally arrived.

Avery forced herself to push back the doom and

gloom. She had always been a tall and broad woman with a firm rack. She laughed aloud, knowing that would change soon, too. It was a reality she accepted because it was for her child. The promise of him or her was worth a few pounds and stretch marks. She'd always been a large woman, always accepted her height and girth. Keeping her old confidence level was imperative.

The express package came the following afternoon, ripping away any idea of being left alone by him. She read the papers a third time, hoping she was reading them wrong.

With a first perfunctory glance, she read his note, reminding her of their dinner date. The next page was a laboratory report. It read that while he had an extremely low count, it was still a viable count. His little swimmers were healthy and hearty if not the normal quantity. She was oddly relieved to read that, the idea of further genetic testing put to rest. What she assumed would be the release papers behind it turned out to be anything but.

"Affidavit of Proxy Marriage" stared at her from the legal-looking Australian document. Avery let out a scream and picked up the closest thing to her. For a second she almost smashed the coffee cup against the wall but relented. Anger wouldn't help her, especially now. Instead, she forced herself to breathe deeply and called her lawyer, only to be informed he was away for the long Presidents weekend and unless it was an absolute emergency, he'd get back to her on Tuesday.

Great, just great, she thought. It was Thursday afternoon and she was to see Mitch the next night. Avery thought through her options and came up blank. He'd trapped her, but only for the weekend, until she could get her lawyer to handle it. In the mean time, she used her on-line connection to research proxy marriages as best she could. It was a mind boggling process considering New York law versus Australian law. Avery raged as she shut down the computer, vowing to make Mitch pay all her legal fees for dissolving his stupid proxy marriage, if it was legal.

"He's got some nerve!" she said aloud to nobody but herself. It didn't help later that night when she lay awake thinking about their time at the lodge together. It was all quite frustrating to realize the web they'd spun themselves into. And she wanted a few of her own questions answered. Especially the main one about Alexandra and her hold over Michael Mitchell Hamilton. Her Mr. Amazed. Well he was about to be amazed by her.

****

Mitch showered quickly in his hotel room, knowing not to keep Avery waiting. He'd spent the last days both elated and depressed. The idea of fathering her child at first seemed like a terrible joke to pull on him, yet every time he thought about it, and he had little else on his mind, he knew she wouldn't name him if she hadn't honestly thought it true.

The test was simple enough; it just annoyed him that he had to wait until he'd arrived in Scotland to have the test performed. He had it done twice, three days apart just to make sure. The results stunned him. He fathered a child, Avery Lambert's baby, and he knew one thing: she'd run as far from him now as she could. His only aim was to keep her with him long enough to make her see his perspective and, hopefully, accept it.

He dispensed with business quickly, attending to it as a nuisance, and flew home to talk to his mother. She was the one who had joked about making it a done deal and then talking it through. She'd gone on to tell him to take her to Las Vegas and marry her quickly. They could spend the rest of their lives fighting about it, but at least her grandchild would have two parents. The idea was crazy; he'd never get Avery to agree to go back to Las Vegas with him.

But his mind kept working overtime and it wasn't until the next evening, it hit him. He was scanning television channels instead of sleeping and caught an old western movie about bringing women across the wilderness to meet prospective grooms in the gold rush era. The thought struck him and made him laugh aloud.

When he finished laughing at himself, he picked up his cell phone and called his lawyer. While they discussed the idea and the legalities of it, they both decided an Australian proxy marriage, one that didn't technically exist, would throw her for a few days and hopefully buy him some time to talk to her.

On the last leg of the trip to New York he thought about her with a huge grin plastered on his face. If he'd been stopped for speeding, the stupid look would get him arrested for being punch drunk. He'd lost four months and he refused to lose any more. He'd been ready to ask her to marry him before this situation started; now knowing she carried his child only intensified his need to be with her all the time.

Chapter Two

He remembered everything about their time together during the drive to Manhattan. He saw her in his mind's eye, her back to him, and her voice husky as she spoke to the contractor in Italian, surprising the man by answering his mumbled words. He stood just outside the open hallway door with his hand poised ready to knock announcing his arrival when he heard the conversation from inside. The heated attitude of the participants made him pause and listen. A male voice used an intimidating tone.

"Ms. Lambert, nobody cares about those numbers. The doors fit and that's the end of the subject."

"No, Mr. Kent, it's not!"

The female voice seemed unaffected by the man's overbearing tone, rather only annoyed by it.

"Those numbers you were given have a purpose. Once the marble flooring goes in and then the throw rugs, the doors won't swing freely. If it's left as it is now, you'll have to take the doors down, re-size them, re-finish them, and then re-hang them. Isn't it much simpler to handle the situation now rather than later when it becomes a problem?"

"It's not my problem. The doors fit."

Mitch didn't hold back any longer listening; he moved to the doorway and watched the confrontation. His purpose in stopping by the site today was to get a first hand look at Ms. Avery Lambert in action, and it seemed he'd picked a perfect time. His first sight of her wasn't what he expected. He watched as she dragged her hand through the top of her long, dark hair in exasperation.

"Is this your initial on this page?" The man only nodded his head. "Then you remember the day we went over these numbers and you signed off that you understood the importance. Next time you should try listening instead of appeasing. The doors won't fit once the carpets are in place and I won't have them being sanded and refinished in this space once the painting has been completed. Please fix them according to the spec sheet as earlier decided and agreed upon."

She stood to her full height before the aging, rotund man and inhaled deeply. As she did, her chest pushed forward even farther than her hour glass figure already did on its own. She wore faded denim overalls and a white shirt underneath. Technically, she was covered in old work clothes, but Mitchell had never seen a workman fill them out quite so exquisitely.

She drew a second deep breath, her breasts rising higher as if to taunt the man standing beside her. Mitch realized the tips of his thumbs were rubbing against his index fingers, as if he could feel her nipple harden between them. A shiver ran through him and landed at his crotch.

"A little sanding's no problem..."

"Yes, it will be."

He leaned against the door frame and watched how she handled the contractor.

"This conversation would go a lot smoother, Mr. Kent, if you could either look at my face or the plans when we speak, not my breasts."

While her tone was tense, she wasn't backing down from his leering look; in fact she was challenging him. It was Mr. Kent whose face turned red and he groaned several incomprehensible words under his breath in a foreign language. It was Mr. Kent who reddened further when she answered him back in the same language.

The stunned man looked at her for all of three seconds before turning on his heel and grabbing the sheet from the makeshift table they'd been standing in front of. He continued to mumble in Italian, Mitch realized after hearing more of the words, and she hollered back an answer. Mr. Kent paused but didn't turn around again; he called one of his workmen over and apparently instructed him to take down the offending doors. He saw that she waited to smile until both men were gone from her view and then turned back to the plans laid before her.

From the back she was just as impressive, her hips filling out the denim in all the right places. He knew she wasn't a small or petite woman by any means. She stood at least five-foot-eight or ten and that was rare for most women he met. It was a habit with him to silently measure women by their height; his six-foot-six frame forced him to measure them before letting himself be carried away by their beauty. Mitchell hated to slouch and a short woman beside him always made him feel like a giant. He liked a tall woman on his arm and in his bed. And Avery Lambert filled the bill, along with her curves in all the right places. After listening to her conversation and ultimate win over the contractor, he held a new respect for the woman he'd come to surprise.

In reality he'd been the one surprised. He expected a slim, tiny woman and before him stood a goddess of his size and proportions. Her breasts would spill out of even his large palms and her hips would fill his grasp when he pulled her to him. Mitch took a breath and shook off the image of him standing behind her, taking her with abandon. She was sturdy and he could use his size to his advantage. She'd take his thrusts and push for more. Mitch made a silent bet with himself that she actually ate meals rather than living on salads as most of the women he knew did.

****

Avery shook her head and went back to the drawing in front of her, muttering her own phrases under her breath in Italian. Her hand automatically dragged her hair from her eyes and she paused to search for an elastic band in her pocket. She straightened and pulled the length of her hair back from her face, separating it into three sections. Her fingers worked quickly and competently to tame the long curls into the braid. Almost finished, she heard a noise behind her.

Turning to see who it was clearing his throat, her hands stilled behind her head when she saw him. Deep brown eyes and dark brown-black hair stared down at her from what had to be close to seven feet of extremely well-put-together man. Her breath halted as she quickly took in the squared jaw and the full lips that centered his face. His shoulders were broad, almost as wide as the doorway, and his waist trim. His legs were long and his thighs strong, straining against the material of his well-cut suit. Right down to his hand-made shoes without a spot of dust.

"Oh, my," Avery thought to herself and felt a rush of adrenaline she hadn't felt in years. She knew he'd been watching her but she didn't know for how long. And she didn't know who he was or why he was there. Slowly, her fingers completed their task and wound the elastic around the ends before she dropped the braid down her back. He watched her the entire time and she refused to turn away first.

"Can I help you?" She spoke in a strong tone, clear and concise if not a little husky.

"I'm here to see the apartment. I'm a friend of

Jack's; he told me to stop by when I could to see what he was having done with the place."

"Oh," was all she managed at first. She forced herself to drag her gaze away from his and turned back to the drawings before continuing. "I'm Avery Lambert, Jack's designer. And you are?" She wiped her sweaty palms on her hips and with a breath turned around to face him again, hoping to keep her hormones in check this time. With his hand extended towards her, he moved easily into the space, his long legs closing the distance in a few paces.

"I'm amazed," he answered. He took her hand in his and held it for just a second too long to be just a business greeting. His eyes locked on hers and she again didn't look away. She studied him as he studied her.

"Well, Mr. Amazed, had you seen the apartment before we started?"

"Yes." He reluctantly pulled his hand from hers and moved farther into the bright, curtain-less room. "I saw it just after he bought the place." He moved to the windows and ran his hand over the moldings stripped down to the bare wood. "There must have been five coats of paint on these." He talked with his back to her, his attention on the wood and glass before him.

"Eight actually: five shades of white, one eggshell, and the first two were original, a pale varnish over the natural wood."

"This took a lot of man hours. Have you done the whole apartment or just this room?"

"We did it all. If you're a friend of Jack's then you know he wouldn't stand for anything less."

He took several steps back and viewed the whole wall. He glanced at her and then his eyes shifted to the floors. "This was painted black," he started, bending down to pull back a length of the protective paper that had been laid down. With only a corner exposed, he saw the floors had been sanded to raw wood, the oak parquet pattern stunning even in its unfinished status. "You'll stain these, I suppose?"

"Yes, just tinted lightly to even out the color then lots of layers of wax and poly to finish. By the time I'm done, a gymnasium could move in here and not ever hurt them, unless of course they paint them again!" She smiled and almost let out a laugh. "So, Mr. Amazed, you approve?"

He laughed back at her use of his non-name but didn't correct her.

"I do." He moved past her to stick his head into the remaining rooms. When he returned, she'd gone back to the pages in front of her. Moving beside her, it was apparent he knew he was crowding her and waited to see how she handled him. In a conspirator's voice, he told her, "Kent's taking down the bathroom doors."

"I didn't expect anything less." Her confidence was steadfast.

"And I'm sure cursing him back in his native language didn't hurt."

His smile made her take a step back, her eyes wary of him. Okay, she decided, he's gorgeous and tall, and he hasn't given me his name on purpose, twice now. Just who is he? Instead of verbalizing her question, when she spoke she asked, "Just how long were you standing in the doorway, Mr. Amazed?"

Her arms folded across her ample chest, well, actually lower, really across her stomach. "Long enough, Ms. Lambert. I like your style."

"Thank you, I think, although I don't think I want to clarify it any further just now. Do you have any questions about the renovation? I was just heading out." He watched as she gathered drawings and samples and neatly stacked them.

"Hundreds," he told her, leaning his head down just a few inches, his lips close to her ear. Several strands had already pulled from the confines of her quick braid and moved against her cheek when he spoke. "But not about this renovation."

He waited for her reaction and only got a startled look. She narrowed her eyes at him, the silky chocolate brown staring at him in disbelief. He took her by surprise and let his lips move to hers, capturing her just before she would have pulled back. His large hand moved behind her head and angled her towards him, pulling her to him, watching her eyes until their lips met. Her hands came up to his chest, flattened against him and started to push him away. Only his gaze made her stop, for just a breath, before he let his eyes slip closed as he savored her mouth.

He didn't push against her or bite at her; he simply let his lips touch hers, to sample them with his own. His tongue brushed at her bottom lip and she automatically let her mouth drop open slightly for him. He didn't plunder her mouth, he teased her lips as he tasted her, sampled her like a rare vintage. His fingers relaxed their grip on her head but didn't pull away. Avery understood he was letting her decide, and she did.

She let her eyes close and she allowed him to kiss her. She swept her tongue against the tip of his and he let out a small groan, spurring her on to deepen her attentions. Her fingers contracted against his chest, the material of his suit jacket crushing beneath them as she pulled him towards her. There was a loud noise in another room and Avery jerked away from him, the back of her hand rising to cover her thoroughly kissed lips as her eyes met his.

Neither said a word and after what seemed like hours he simply smiled and left. That was it; he just turned and walked away, leaving her stunned by her actions and his. She still had no idea who he was or why he was really there. All she knew was that this tall, dark stranger had made her feel something she'd known was missing for a long time. She'd just never understood it on such a basic level before.

The mumbled Italian words meant nothing to the outsider, only a grumble of language. Avery knew what she was saying, she was wondering where her sanity went. On another level she understood instantly, this total stranger made her feel female. Not frilly feminine which she'd never be; rather he seemed to appreciate her in erotic ways. And now she knew she'd fit against him in all the right places.

****

Mitchell stood stock still in the elevator waiting for his body to calm down and his erection to recede. Ms. Avery Lambert wasn't what he'd bargained for on many fronts, especially a sexual one. He'd have to think very carefully before he went any further. A brunette beauty who held her own next to him was a new experience. By the time he reached the sidewalk, his body had calmed, but every time he thought of her for days after, he'd tingle slightly, leaving him with an ache to touch her again. Letting go of restraints with Avery would allow him to get primal, no more holding back because he feared his size would intimidate a woman. He sensed she'd match him stroke for stroke and probably ask for more.

Chapter Three

Avery stood to the side of the room smiling at assorted faces, some she knew and others she didn't. She held a glass of chilled wine in her hand, and studied the responses of the invited guests as they toured the completed apartment. Jack had been thrilled with the renovation and she was quite happy with the end result herself.

It was a mix of open, comfortable contemporary and turn-of-the-century hardwoods. While all the original wood floors, windows, and mill work had been lovingly restored, they'd added an eclectic mix of ultra modern and antique pieces to tie it all together. His art collection contained a mix showing another side of its owner. Somehow it all worked for her and she was glad it was done.

Ever since that strange day months before, she hadn't felt comfortable in the space. No, she corrected herself, it wasn't uncomfortable, it was a feeling of being on edge. She'd never see him again and she hadn't wanted to ask Jack who he was. She tried to forget the tall, dark stranger who kissed her with such tenderness and authority.

Just thinking of him now sent a chill down her spine and landed in a heat that centered her. It infuriated her to think how one kiss could make her feel erotic even months later. And it annoyed her that every man she'd come in contact with since her little interlude with Mr. Amazed had been measured against him and summarily dismissed. At this rate she'd never find a partner or a mate. Instead, she'd be haunted by the phantom of a man who was too good to be true. She let out a sigh and turned towards the entry only to find him leaning against the door frame watching her.

She stilled under his scrutiny, held her place, and watched him. It was Mr. Amazed who finally broke the stand-off and entered the apartment. Berating herself for the case of nerves he inspired, Avery forced her shoulders back and stood tall as he made his way across to her. His long legs didn't give her much time to prepare and he stood beside her too quickly.

"You've done quite a job, Ms. Lambert. I approve," he said, watching her intently from under thick dark lashes. "And Mr. Kent, did he survive the experience?"

She laughed even when she tried not to and his smile just about pushed her senses over the edge. It lit up his dark face, as if she were the only one in the room and his smile was just for her. He wore a dark blue suit with a starched white shirt. The top buttons of his collar were open and his tie was conspicuously absent. Even his scent excited her. He smelled of soap and man. It was a heady combination.

Something about this man made her think outside the norm, instantly recognizing the pros and cons. Avery learned a long time ago you couldn't have everything just because you wanted it. There was always a price to pay, some of them heavier than others. His smile would be her undoing. His confidence excited her. Instinct told her to be careful. He was a powerful man in many ways and she knew nothing about him, not even his name.

****

Mitchell watched her for a long time from the doorway. He'd spotted her immediately upon entering the apartment. It would be hard to miss her, especially tonight; in heels and a red dress, with her dark hair bundled on top of her head, she was the goddess of his boyhood dreams and the vision he carried in his head each day since meeting her. She'd haunted him, literally. His mind was overrun with her, all the time. A tall woman would trigger her memory; a dark-haired woman would remind him of their kiss.

Tonight, standing beside her dressed in red, he knew she would inhabit him forever. Her smile stripped away any defenses he might have held against her. Staring at her, he knew he hadn't enhanced her in his mind as he told himself often. Her eyes were silky pools of milk chocolate against flawless skin, with thick, full lips that were meant to be kissed. They were tinted the same shade as her dress and he found himself wetting his own lips when his throat went dry.

"He survived, but he may retire after this," she said with a laugh. "At least all the doors open easily."

She held his gaze and he knew something was happening between them. Call it chemical or hormonal, or just plain attraction, he was drawn to her in a way he'd never come close to with another woman. If they'd been alone, he would have touched her, drawn his mouth to hers to taste her again. The noise receded to the background, neither acknowledging the crowd around them.

"Jack's happy with the place and he's thrilled with you."

"As long as Jack's happy. After all, he's got to live here."

"What are you working on now?"

"A nursery midtown and an elegant French provincial condo overlooking the park."

He liked that she gave him her full attention, looking him in the eye as they talked. She had a way of making him feel special even in a crowd and he wondered if she realized how much she stood out in the same crowd.

"You don't impress me as the French type."

Avery didn't stifle her laugh and seemed relaxed after releasing it. His eyes flared and he instantly understood the dual meaning of his words. "All right, that wasn't completely accurate, I meant…"

"I know what you meant, but it's what the client wants that counts."

Bold and brazen, she let her finger run along his jaw before adding, "What do you want, Mr. Amazed?" Avery watched his eyes carefully. "Do you know?"

He managed to get, "Yes," out but his voice was tight and controlled. Mitch studied her as she stood beside him. She just felt right. She was a solid woman and fit his personal image of what his woman should look and feel like. It also wasn't lost on him how many eyes gravitated towards her. Self-preservation pushed back the jealous flair that bolted through his being. These strangers were undressing his woman with their eyes and he could do nothing about it.

His eyes wandered the length of her and no further words were needed. He watched her moisten her lips with the tip of her tongue and knew he had to pull himself together. "Show me the rest of the apartment."

His hand moved to her elbow and guided her through the group of people in the main living area. She moved through the dining area and the kitchen quickly, both filled with people. The doorway to the master bedroom was open and the room looked empty but she refused to move into the room with him, rather holding her place in the doorway. He seemed to understand and opened a door to his right.

The office was empty, only the small banker's

light on the far corner of the desk illuminated the space. Mitchell closed the door behind them and leaned against it, his hand reaching down to slip the lock. For long seconds neither said a word. They stared at each other in a mutual gaze.

Avery finally broke the tension. She placed her glass on the desk and moved toward him. His arms opened to her and she walked directly into his embrace. There was no hesitation as his arms closed around her, pulling her to his chest. Her hands went to his face, angling his chin towards her. Mitch wanted this kiss, needed it to stay sane. He didn't care who she was or why she was there, only that he wanted to taste her again, hoping it would break the stupor he'd been in since their first meeting.

Their gazes held as their mouths neared and he watched as she touched her mouth to his and only slipped closed when they made contact. He'd waited months to see her again on purpose. Now that she was this close, he knew he wouldn't let her get away without knowing if it was real or imagined. Mitchell deepened the kiss, taking them both to an unexpected height of desire.

Instead of satisfying his curiosity, she fanned his desires like no other woman before had. Avery pulled back just enough to watch him, study him, before resuming her onslaught against his mouth. Gone was the tender kiss of exploration; in its place, hunger and desire unleashed something buried deep inside. His hands tightened, pulling her against the want she created so easily in him. A soft groan filtered through her lips at the feel of his hardness against her. With each slight movement of her hip he felt her heat, and his mouth told her he more than lusted for her.

Intense as the kiss was, Avery heard voices filtering through from the hallway and moved away quickly, smoothing her dress back into place. She picked up her glass and walked to the far corner of the room, watching his reflection in the window as he slipped open the lock and took the chair behind the desk. Only seconds later the door swung open and a couple poked their heads in.

"Oh, sorry to interrupt," the woman said.

Avery forced one of her best smiles forward, "No problem, it's quiet in here, sound proofed." The two moved into the room and gave it a quick glance.

"Not a bad view if you have to work from home," the man said.

"You bring too much work home with you now. If I gave you a room like this, I'd never see you," the woman teased back, their smiles matching. Avery watched them and smiled. They moved away and only then did she look at him

"Would you like to get out of here? I'm sure we could find some place without all these interruptions."

"Jack would be offended if I left so early," she started. "And I don't even know your name." She shook her head and turned back to the window.

"Does it really matter?" he asked, his voice low and throaty. It said all that needed to be expressed. His voice dripped with lust and want; a voice that told her sex would be anything but ordinary with him.

"Yes, it matters to me. I'm sorry if I gave you the wrong idea. I'd better get back to the party."

He laughed at her and she stilled halfway across the room. "Avery, you want me as much as I want you. Why not just accept it and see what happens?" He spoke truthfully from his perspective.

"I'd like to, I really would," she whispered.

He rose from the chair and again closed the door. He watched her eyes flash with concern and he stared at her. He didn't lock it this time, only leaned against it again.

"Please let me by."

It wasn't a plea, it was a command. He noticed

the change in her body language: her shoulders set back, her stance ready for confrontation. "I hope we'll meet again one day, Ms. Lambert." He moved away from the door and leaned one hip on the corner of the desk. "Red is definitely your color." Again he gazed at her from head to toe, taking in the red wrap dress that clung to every curve and left a long expanse of leg below it. His appraisal had him hard and ready, a response long forgotten.

"Thank you," she answered before asking what she really wanted to know. "Why won't you tell me your name?"

He didn't hesitate with his answer; rather he told her the truth in clear and concise language, leaving no doubt to his intentions. "Because it won't matter tomorrow. I'll be gone and won't be back in the city for months. I'm not looking for a relationship of any kind, especially one that's long distance. I'm single and I plan to stay that way. If you're interested in an evening to explore our mutual attraction, I'm all for it. We're both consenting adults and you have a choice to make." He watched her while he spoke, his eyes daring her to change her mind.

"Had that little speech all ready and memorized did you?" She threw her head back and laughed at him. What she did next surprised him. She moved to a chair beside the desk and sat, pausing only to pull off her shoes. "All right, Mr. Amazed," she began. "So you're only out for one evening's good time. I'm sorry but that's not my style. Case closed. But I'm curious. Can we talk or would you rather join the party and find a willing partner so your evening won't be a total waste?"

"By all means, let's talk." He moved to the large chair behind the desk and she laughed at him again.

"Defensive move?" she challenged.

"Definitely."

"Are you always so brazen and forward? When

you see a woman who interests you do you just kiss her to see if there will be sparks?"

"No, generally not. I assume it would get my face slapped quite often." His eyes told her he was definitely serious.

"Yes, I agree. So why me?" Avery watched him settle in the chair, sipping from her glass to hide the smile she was trying to hold back.

"You tempted my common sense?"

"Somehow I don't see you as the type to lose control, at least not that easily."

"Usually not, but..."

He left the statement open ended and she decided to finish it for him.

"Did you have a bad marriage and have sworn off it for eternity or are a child of divorce?" Avery pulled the other chair towards her and propped her legs up on it, the expanse of thigh lengthening to his vision.

His hands itched to touch her and he moved them to the arms of the chair. "Neither. Reasonably stable family home, no ex-wives lurking in the background to bleed me dry." His smile was just short of smug.

It had been a long time since she met a man to verbally spar with.

"No, you'd never accept that. So, what, you're heart was crushed and broken when you were just a tender lad and you never want to hurt like that again?" She was enjoying teasing him. He went from relaxed and casual to edgy and tense before her eyes. "So, are you just afraid of commitment or are you a cross-dresser and you don't want to share your wardrobe? Or are you a trans-sexual?"

Finally he burst out laughing and she joined him, enjoying the release of the sexual tension filtering in the air around them. It allowed them both to settle back and relax in the situation.

"Would you like another drink? If I'm going to

bare all my secrets, I know I'll need one." Truer words had never left his lips. Avery was a woman who kept him on edge and he liked the challenge she offered. He stood and turned towards the door, waiting for her answer.

"Are you sure you're not trying to ply me with wine so I'll change my mind?"

"No, just thirst. You've made your choice I won't push you. But I would like to spend some time with you. I'll be right back," he told her as he slipped from the room. He glanced back and caught her fanning herself.

Mitch slipped through the party goers and confidently appraised Jack's wine selections. He grabbed a white that was crisp and dry, knowing he chose it because it would remind him of Avery the next time he tasted it. Schooling himself, he faced the idea that she wasn't to be his. While depressing, Mitch knew ultimately it would be best.

What he had in mind would only complicate their relationship and Avery was a complicated woman on her own. The added stress of a personal relationship would make their working arrangement difficult to say the least. She was the first woman he'd met that made him start to rethink his position in life. Although he knew the basics of his life wouldn't change, he resigned himself to getting to know her from a distance.

He returned quickly, two fresh glasses in one hand and a full bottle of white wine in the other. He poured for them both and took the seat behind the desk again. "First, let's settle a few things, all right?" She nodded and he continued. "I'm not a transsexual or cross-dresser."

"What a shame, for a moment I though I'd found a new shopping buddy. I know all the best tall ladies stores in town," she told him with a wink over her glass. "And I was already fantasizing about the contents of your closet!"

He raised an eyebrow at her and she laughed at him easily, almost daring him to continue. "I've not had my heart broken beyond repair, yet, and I'm not looking for it to be a new experience. My reasons are quite simple. I believe in marriage and home and children, the whole package," he paused. "But not for me."

"What holds you apart from the rest of us looking for the perfect life we've been brought up to expect, only to find it doesn't truly exist?"

Mitchell leaned back in his seat and decided he'd tell her the truth, mostly just to see her reaction. Avery wasn't one-night-stand material and he respected her for not changing her principles for him, even though ultimately it's what he wanted. Most often women didn't push for more information. They were interested or not and Mitch had never been asked to justify his perspective. She intrigued him and he decided to carefully enjoy their time together.

"I said marriage and children. I'm sterile, Avery, so it's never been an option for me. I've known since I was very young that I wouldn't have a family of my own. I've tailored my life around the idea. I've been extremely lucky with business and that's probably because I only had myself to disappoint if I took a wrong step. Most women, whether they admit it up front or not, want some semblance of a normal family, eventually, in their lives. I can't provide that. Therefore, I don't create a situation that would only harm two people in the end." The silence that followed his gallant statement was long but not uncomfortable. He watched as she seemed to be processing the information he gave her.

"What about adoption? There are alternatives?"

"Yes, there are, only I learned long ago that I'm a very selfish man. I don't know if I could love another man's child and since the test has never been placed before me, I can't answer you honestly. I can only tell you that so far, I haven't met a woman who I really felt would want to spend her life with me under these circumstances."

"There are an awful lot of women out there who can't bear children. Why not with a woman who's in the same state of mind, childless and not afraid to let the world see she's not defeated by it. Instead, like you, she chooses to live a full and varied life."

"Women truly are a breed unto themselves, Avery. I know what I'm capable of; I haven't found a woman I'd be compatible with for a long-term relationship. Don't get me wrong, I'm not out filling my nights with an endless parade of women that I use and then toss away. Rather, I've always understood and accepted the differences between societies in general and what it offered me."

"And what if that somehow changed?" She handed him her glass for a refill and slipped back into her seat. "Modern medicine being what it is, if you could reverse history?"

"Unknown. Not going to happen. What about you? Didn't you always know somewhere deep inside you that you were mother material, just that you would choose your time carefully so you could have a career and children when the time was right?"

"Yes, absolutely. I've been careful with my choices and have built a career for myself with a family in mind. A career that is flexible enough to allow me that privilege when the time is right."

"Which is why we're sharing a bottle of Jack's private stock instead of making mad, passionate love on the sofa with the party locked out behind that door."

"So sure of yourself, I think I would have preferred a more personal environment."

"Ah, the romantic. Candles and firelight, the stage all set to get you in the mood."

"Sometimes, yes, but there's something to be said for quick release on the living room floor or kitchen counter. It's the crowd I could do without. Do you need the idea of an audience or being caught to get erect?" She watched his eyes flash at her and laughed. "God, you're so easy."

"No, never easy, Avery." His tone sobered her.

"No, I don't suppose you would be. Is that why you hold back, and why you chase away the possibilities with your canned speech and outrageous tactics? Was I supposed to be shocked by you?"

"No. I learned a long time ago it's easier to lay my cards on the table. That way nobody gets hurt. If you chose to spend time with me, you'd go into it knowing what you'd get from me. We'd have a good time, Avery. I travel a great deal with my work and I'm not averse to having companionship on those trips. I live large and fast, and I'm willing to share it with a woman." His eyes again offered her his invitation.

"As long as she stays in the neat little compartment you've put her in. She's not to overstep her bounds and ask for anything beyond the deal, is that it?"

"Nobody gets hurt that way when it ends, and, Avery, it always ends."

"Do you really get a lot of women this way?" There was no humor to her words. It was a serious question and she wanted a serious answer.

"No, but the ones I spend time with know what to expect from me and, knowing ahead of time, it saves us both a lot of misunderstandings and grief. Sooner or later one or both of us tires and wants to move on. I prefer to go as a gentleman, not a cad who alluded to promises never meant to be kept."

"I do understand how you're so successful; you have nothing to look forward to so it's all a crap shoot to you. If you lose a deal, you move on. It's the same with women. You bore easily, don't you?"

He laughed at her and she pulled her legs from

the other seat and slipped her feet into her high-heeled shoes.

"Are we done?" he asked, watching her put her shoes on. "I've made you uncomfortable?" He hadn't thought she'd give up so easily, and was almost disappointed that she'd walk away now, just when they were actually having a meaningful conversation.

Chapter Four

His tone alone wouldn't let her run from him even if that was her intention. She'd stand her ground with him and maybe push him back a step or two, just on general principle.

"No. I was going to slip into the kitchen and see if I could find us something to snack on before the wine goes to my head, unless you'd rather rejoin the others?" Her dare was sweetly spoken but received and acknowledged by the lift of his left eyebrow.

"By all means. I don't want to be responsible for your hangover tomorrow. I'll wait for you here." His look said so much more but she wasn't willing think about it now.

"That almost sounded like a threat," she told him as she exaggerated her swaying hips walking toward the door. "Any preferences?"

"Whatever you can find. Surprise me."

"I just might at that, Mr. Amazed." Avery opened the door; the noise of the party filtered into the room and was shut out just as quickly.

She used the time away from him to let her heart stop pounding and to give herself a pep talk. She detoured into the kitchen and took a small sampling of the tasty items being offered while rationalizing that she'd been preoccupied by him for months. The best way to get him out of her head was to spend some time with him. The illusion would be broken and she could leave the consuming thoughts of him behind, and she decided to keep the memory of him and his kisses in their proper perspective.

It wasn't long before she returned to their private spot. Mitchell hadn't moved from his seat and watched her enter with a small tray. Party food covered one side and cheese chunks with fruit the other. It was what she had wrapped in a cloth napkin that caused him to cock his left eyebrow. Avery laid the small tray on the desk between them and went back to her chosen seat, again slipping off her shoes as she settled. "There's quite a party going on outside that door. Are you sure you'd rather be locked away in here with a dead issue?" He reached for a slice of cheese and took several of the tart green grapes at the same time. Avery watched his hands intently, knowing his strong fingers would do wonderful things to her. They were long and thick, working man's hands, yet she knew they would be gentle when he wanted them to be. Her eyes slid up to his and she knew he'd been watching her. She felt the heat rise in her cheeks and accepted her defeat.

"All right, I admit I'm attracted to you. I wouldn't have let you kiss me either time if I wasn't. And just because we've laid our cards out doesn't mean I can't wonder what it might have been like."

"Why wonder, as long as you know I'll literally be gone by seven tomorrow morning. Why not sample?" His lips turned into a mischievous grin which Avery promptly called him on.

"And does that look work for you often?"

"On occasion. I will admit you're not the average woman I meet. Maybe that's why I'm in here with you instead of out there."

"Nope, you like me because I'm tall with curves." He nodded in agreement. "That's fine, I know what I am. I'm a large woman of five-foot-nine and I happen to have an hour-glass figure. I had to decide a long time ago if my body image would defeat me in life. I've never been referred to as skinny or even thin.

But I have great legs and hips, and my breasts are all my own. And since gravity hasn't taken over yet, I'm content to be what I am, a large woman with a firm rack." Avery laughed at him and he understood.

"That's it, you know. Why I'm here. You're one of the few women I've ever met who is comfortable in her own skin. And that, Ms. Lambert, is a compliment I've rarely spoken."

Suddenly there was an intensity between them. He understood her; take me as I am, because I'm not going to change for you. He understood because it was the major rule he'd lived his life by.

She nodded and whispered, "Thank you." It was Mitchell that turned away. "Well, you just earned your bonus." Avery drew a deep breath and pulled the cloth napkin to the center of the desk, making a production of uncovering its contents. She glanced up at him and asked, "You won't tell Jack?" A mischievous smile formed on her lips and he watched the tip of her tongue moisten her bottom lip in anticipation of the hidden morsel.

"Promise. What did you find?"

"I know some of his hiding places too," she said triumphantly as she pulled back the last bit of cloth to reveal six perfect, milk chocolate-covered, double-stuffed sandwich cookies. Mitchell laughed aloud and pushed back in his chair after taking one from the pile. He bit into it and savored the flavors that mingled on his tongue.

"You, Ms. Lambert, are a rare woman indeed. How did you find his stash?"

"Easy. He's conventional in some ways."

"The wine closet?" She nodded as she took the last bite of her cookie.

"Cool and dry."

"Are you going to give me away? By the way, how do you know Jack?" He watched her take a second cookie and push back in her seat. "Or are you a con man who infiltrated his party?"

"Avery, you have an amazing mind. You got it on the first try. I'm a bum, really, sponging off rich friends, hoping to meet women who will take care of me for a few months in return for lavishing them with my personal attentions." He glanced over at her and smiled.

"Is it a tiring profession, always having to perform on demand, so to speak?"

Mitchell was laughing when the door swung open, light and noise spilling into the room, along with Jack and several other people. His blue eyes took in the scene in front of him and Jack laughed. He crossed to Mr. Amazed and enveloped him in a bear hug.

"I never saw you come in, but I should have figured you'd zero in on Avery." She watched as the men pulled back and smiled. "It's been a long time, Mitch. Good to see you. And apparently you already know Avery."

"The place looks great, Jack. I was sidetracked immediately," he said, glancing over his shoulder at her.

"And it looks like you've found my private stash! Which one of you was it?"

Right on cue, both Avery and Mitch turned to each other and said, "He did," and "She did," which made Jack laugh harder.

"How long will you be in town?"

"Only until tomorrow morning."

"I'll be on the coast in about two weeks; we'll set something up for then."

"Leave the weekend open and we'll go up to the lodge."

"Done. I'll have my assistant confirm the dates. It will give me something to look forward to." Jack hesitated and gave Mitch a sidelong glance. "You'll stock the pond this time?" He turned to Avery and told her of his last trip when Mitch apparently convinced Jack that the pond was full and he was just a terrible fisherman.

"I've got to get back out there, although I'd much rather stay in here with you two." He walked to Avery and kissed her on both cheeks. "You did a great job, kid."

"Thank you, kind sir. It's all in who I'm working for."

"I'm going to have to move to get to see you again," Jack teased.

"Give it a year or so; I'm booked until then." She winked at him as he turned from the doorway.

"Enjoy," he tossed out then stopped. "Mitch, I like Avery."

"Yes, so do I, and it seems I amuse her. She's having a wonderful time busting my chops over my approach." They watched each other relax.

"I should have had more faith in you, Avery. You've got his number." He left, closing the door behind him, and the noise and light faded. Avery and Mitch were silent for a while.

"All right, so you really know Jack and apparently aren't sponging off him. And now I have a name to put with the face. Mitchell. Do you prefer Mitchell or Mitch? Both would suit, I think." She studied him, appraising his name with his appearance. "Yes, both suit you. Mitchell when you're angry and demanding and Mitch when I want to get your attention."

"You're having way too much fun with all this."

"I know. I assumed tonight would be like most of the housewarmings I attend."

"Happy to be of service," he replied. "I somehow like the idea of being your evening's entertainment."

"I'm sorry I'm not turning out to be yours."

****

The conviction in her words echoed through his mind and landed straight at his erection. He shifted in his seat and pulled the chair closer to the wood surface, effectively covering his current state. The position also closed the distance between them. He stretched his hand across the desk; she hesitated only for a second before dropping her hand onto his, his fingers closing over hers.

"So, tell me, Avery, who will the perfect man be for you?" She eyed him but didn't take back her hand.

"Someone who's clear on their ideals of love and marriage, monogamous. Someone who wants to attempt the dream, family and home and all the craziness that goes with it. Someone who'll understand that not every day will be easy and he'll still want to come home to be with me to make it better. Someone who laughs easily and uses common sense. I want a man who will love and accept me just for me. He'll accept that there are things about each of us that can't be changed and be willing to accept reality.

"Someone who's with me not for what I do, or how I look; someone who'll realize that when I commit myself it will be with my full heart and soul. I don't see any other way to make it work." Avery glanced to Mitch and back to their clasped hands. She closed her eyes for just a second and drew a deep breath.

Mitch watched from under his lashes and his heart twisted. Knowing they were getting entirely too deep, Mitch whispered, "And he has to be hung like a horse." He watched for her reaction and breathed a sigh of relief when she finally smiled at him.

"That goes without saying. He'll have to adore me and lavish my body with all his masculine powers at my whim."

"That goes without saying." Seemingly reluctant, she slipped her hand from his and sat back. He did the same, understanding their time was ending. He knew he was right when she slipped her shoes back on. Mitch didn't want to sound desperate but he didn't want their time to end. "How about going somewhere for coffee and then I'll take you home?" Her eyes flew to his and he knew she'd reject him.

"Thanks, Mitch. But to be totally honest with you, you tempt my common sense and that's dangerous. I misjudged you. I now appreciate you letting me know the score in advance. While I can say I've never had a man put it all out there quite the way you did, I do appreciate you giving me the choice." She looked at him before continuing.

"If I hadn't known, I would have been disappointed after. Quite honestly, I've spent enough of the last few months thinking about the way you kissed me the last time we met. If you made love to me, I'd never get you out of my head. And that would be dangerous for me and uncomfortable for you. Thank you for your honesty. You'll have to understand I can't allow you to take me home."

Mitch nodded his understanding. He stood, pausing before deciding what to do. He walked quickly towards the door to meet her there. His hands went to her shoulders and she moved against him, her hands at his waist, her head resting on his shoulder. They held each other for a long time, both reluctant to end the embrace. His hand skimmed her back and she stroked his sides and back with her trimmed nails through the cloth of his shirt.

She felt his arousal against her and didn't move against him; instead she stilled in his arms until he pulled back. "Mitch?" she asked, daring to look to him.

His left hand circled her waist and brought her to him, his right slid up her spine to rest behind her head, cradling her at the angle he wanted. His mouth touched hers lightly but it wasn't enough. Avery's hands slipped up his back, pulling him tighter to her, crushing her breasts against his chest. His left hand dropped lower, pulling her hips against his desire and moving her over him.

Her demands on his mouth became greater and he gave her what he thought she wanted. He took what he'd dreamt about, accepted how right she felt in his arms. Their desire was apparent and somehow intensified by knowing it wouldn't be fulfilled. They mutually demanded the surrender of the other.

Mitch kissed her as if his breath was drawn from her, absorbing her into him. Avery apparently wanted to punish him for being forbidden to her and she ground against him. Mitch groaned and pulled away from her mouth, their intensity almost overwhelming to him.

"Avery…I want you," he whispered, his lips on her forehead.

"I want you, too, in a way I've never felt before. You scare me, Mitch." She rose up on her toes and placed a light kiss against his lips. "I don't think I'll forget you, Mr. Amazed. You've shown me what I've been searching for is out there."

"I'd only end up hurting you, Avery."

"I know, Mitch. That's why I'm going home, alone." Neither moved away and they held on. "If I met you a few years ago, we might have had some fun."

"It's one possibility; the other is that you would have found me brash and insensitive."

"Possibly. I suppose we can't second guess it. I accept that we weren't meant to be, even though I'm drawn to you."

"I know the feeling, Avery."

"Good luck Mitch," she whispered and finally pulled from the warmth of his embrace.

"Avery, don't settle." She shook her head and stepped into the hallway.

****

Mitchell remained in the den for another hour

before he ventured back to the party. It was thinning down and he easily slipped away from the crowd. He walked back to his hotel, Avery's perfume embedded in his memory. The way she felt in his arms and the passion she exuded with her kiss. The way her body moved with even ordinary movements. She'd branded herself on his brain and now he wondered if his best-laid plans wouldn't come back to haunt him.

She hadn't mentioned the hotel offer to him or Jack, only teased she'd be busy for the next year. At several different times during the evening he thought to tell her his last name but didn't. Each time something stopped him from revealing the information. He knew if he had, she wouldn't accept the bid.

He had known months before, when he decided to put her on the short list of designers to take on his "high roller" suites, that she would be different in her approach. He still wanted to see what approach she'd come up with, wondering about the validity of actually hiring her and not telling her who he was. If he stayed away from the site when she was around…If he missed the first meetings…But she was a smart woman; she'd eventually figure it out.

He was just turning the corner in front of his hotel and he smiled to himself, wishing he could see her face when she found out her trip to Las Vegas next week was to meet with him.

Chapter Five

Avery sat in the impressive board room of the Hamilton Hotel in downtown Las Vegas and looked at the other two designers who had been asked to bid on the new Hamilton project. It had been months ago when the letter inviting her to bid had arrived.

A second Hamilton Hotel was being built at the other end of the strip, a sister to the original Hamilton. Her invitation was to design the "high roller" suites. Not available to the general public, these rooms were reserved for players with large credit limits. A person had to be in the high seven digit category to be considered for these palatial spaces. And she knew they had to actually use their credit line during their stay, not just keep a steady balance. She also knew only extremely high profile celebrities, politicians, and some royalty would ever see the spaces she designed.

She was given one month to submit a prospectus and two months dragged on before she heard back. She was then invited to submit a more focused and complete bid. They had given her eight weeks to get her ideas and numbers in line. So here she sat, waiting for the process to begin.

Avery had spent some time in Atlantic City when her invitation first arrived. While she hadn't gained access to the high roller suites at the Hamilton Hotel, Atlantic City, she'd learned a lot about their style during her short stay. She'd used the time to check out the other hotels and casinos to make sure she was clear on the current line of thinking. Learning about the feel and mood of the hotel, its guests and employees, as well as the town around her, she was able to incorporate both into her concept for the Hamilton II suites in Las Vegas.

Her first competitor was an older woman with a slim frame and impeccable taste in clothes and jewels. Hailing from San Francisco, she was polite but not overly friendly. The second candidate was a middle-aged man, who didn't stand taller than five foot four. Avery had contained a smile when she was introduced to him and he stood before her at nipple height. She liked him immediately after his comment about "breaking the ice in an extraordinary way," which relaxed them both.

While Ms. San Francisco was civil, she wasn't courteous. Her shorter male counterpart was Canadian, his accent thicker at times than others. He was friendly and competent and they easily discussed a layout that had been in a recent trade magazine while they waited.

Bob Matthews entered with a gracious smile and informed them that Mr. Hamilton had seen all of their ideas and would sit in on the meeting by conference call. Avery was somewhat disappointed; she'd wanted to meet the man, Michael M. Hamilton, behind the luxury hotels to sharpen her formal presentation. Now, it seemed, she'd go with her original ideas and let her instinct guide her. The telephone was set up and they all settled around the large table. Avery noticed that while it had video capacity, it wasn't being used for their call today. That intrigued her, especially since the hotel boasted state of the art technology in its casinos.

Ms. San Francisco was asked to go first and they all listened while she described her vision for the suites as covered in silks and satins with a French provincial feel. They would be very formal suites, dripping with gold and gilt, suggesting opulence and outrageous expense. Mr. Hamilton asked several questions after her presentation, signaling to them that they had his full attention. Answering easily, she almost gave the aura of being bored by his second-guessing her.

Avery listened to the man's smooth voice over the speaker and tried to visualize him. He was notorious for never having his photograph taken. He was supposed to be nearing forty and a genius with money. He'd never married and was elusive but not reclusive. Listening to his voice, she thought it strangely soothing.

Mr. Canada took a different approach as his presentation unfolded. He was very much into feng shui, with a definite oriental flavor. Lots of black lacquer and bold colors mixed with white. Avery thought his orchid motif was a little overpowering and overused but didn't offer her opinion. Again, Mr. Hamilton entered the conversation and qualified some of his ideas. His questions were valid and he joked with the designer that maybe they should add on a hothouse for all the orchids they'd need. Mr. Canada was quick to offer information about a wholesale supplier that would cover the problem.

Avery went last and wondered how the order was chosen. This could be good or bad, she decided, wondering if Mr. Hamilton had become bored by the process. She took a deep breath and walked to the front of the room, her red dress giving her confidence. For a second she thought back to her Mr. Amazed and her lips curled into a smile. The last time she'd worn this particular dress was at Jack's housewarming, when Mitch told her it was her color. Her presentation took an entirely different approach.

"I see the high roller suites from another angle," she started, and concisely laid out her plan for four suites, situated away from the main hotel behind private gates. She used compass points to delineate her suites and had turned them toward their corresponding points. This design gave all four suites a private entrance, sheltered even from the other high rollers. Each room would be decorated differently.

After a loud groan from Ms. San Francisco which Avery ignored, she went on to describe each one in detail. North would be modeled after an Adirondack chalet, exposed beams and honeyed log walls. It would be accomplished in bold earth tones, with wood accents. South would have a tropical feel due to its pastel colors and lighter furniture styles. East would have an oriental flair, with only a small amount of lacquer surfaces, using fabric and wall coverings to expand on the theme. Her west suite would be a mix of upscale contemporary. She went on to explain how each room would function and the way a lap pool and private loggia area corresponded with each suite, including privacy issues.

Mr. Hamilton asked several pertinent questions and she was thankful she had an answer for each. When she finally sat back in her seat, Bob Matthews dismissed them with his thanks. They were asked back the next morning for the final decision and told to enjoy the hospitality of the hotel during their stay.

Ms. San Francisco disappeared in a cloud of perfume while Avery and Mr. Canada decided to share lunch. She enjoyed her meal with Norman Ethan and liked his sense of humor. Excusing herself from his afternoon of hitting the tables, she found herself pool side, a book in her hand.

Avery let herself drift in the warm sunshine, confident that the umbrella she sat beneath would shield her from burning. She didn't know how long she dozed in the afternoon heat but she awoke flushed, the remnants of an erotic dream disappearing from her mind. She tried to remember and knew it was no use. Her dream was just as elusive as its main character, her Mr. Amazed.

Avery decided after their last meeting that she was enamored with him simply because she wasn't going to have him. It was an idea she'd entertained often; a simple call to Jack could get his number and a call to Mitch would most likely produce her desired result. But she hadn't asked or made the call, knowing she wanted more for her future. If she got this job, her commission would take away any financial worries she might have in considering her next personal step. A fat nest egg would take away her last stumbling block to becoming a single parent.

It wasn't a decision she had come to lightly. Until her last birthday she had high hopes of meeting Mr. Right to share her future with. Now, almost a year later, she still saw no signs of him on the horizon and she was rethinking her approach. She was confident she could raise a child or two on her own and give them the love she'd stored up all her life. And if she met the right man down the road, he'd accept her and her children or he wouldn't be Mr. Right. The commission loomed in the background and she knew in her mind it was a done deal. If she got this job, she'd complete it and head back to New York, directly to the fertility center she'd chosen from her intense research. She'd spoken with her doctor recently and was comfortable that her body was in good shape, ready to carry and nurture a new life.

****

Mitch watched from across the expanse of the pool area. Covered in a one piece black maillot suit, her long legs propelled her body through the sun-drenched water with ease, her strong arms pulling at the same time. When she moved from the water he hardened at the sight of her as she smoothed back her wet hair and dropped onto the lounge chair. The wet material clung to every curve and told him he'd been right about her.

She was solid and firm, full and rounded, and his hands ached to touch her again. He'd receded into the hotel to take care of business for a few hours and found himself pre-occupied with the knowledge she was soaking up the sun just a short distance away.

"That's about all for today; breakfast is all set for tomorrow morning. Are you sure you don't want to be there?" Bob asked, as he pushed papers into a leather folder and handed them off to an assistant.

"No, it's better this way. Set up the conference call and I'll break the news."

"Your choice," Bob said then watched his friend and boss intently. "She suits you," he added before leaving the room.

Mitch laughed and let him go, not challenging his remarks. How could he, after all, he was right. Avery did suit him. If only she felt the same way about him. If he could give her what he ultimately thought she wanted, he'd never have left her after the housewarming. But his research on her turned up the morsel of information that she'd been interviewing fertility centers and he knew she was a woman who was born to be a parent.

He checked his watch and knew if he was going to approach her; it had to be now, before she went back to her room. He pulled off his tie and dropped it in his pocket, unbuttoning the top two buttons of his shirt before leaving his private office.

****

Avery accepted the frosty Tom Collins the waiter brought her and sipped at the cold concoction, enjoying the tangy flavors. She'd tried to read several times but felt lazy and the book wasn't holding her attention. Instead, she allowed herself to just relax and do nothing but soak up sun. A large body blocked the rays and she looked up to see Mr. Amazed, Mitchell, standing before her.

"Avery, is that you?" he started.

"Mitch?" She sat forward and swung her legs to the side, standing easily beside him. She moved close to him but didn't dare touch him, letting herself stare at him, not believing he was really there. "What are you doing here?" In a flash she realized she was wet from the pool, her hair air drying and her make-up long gone. From the look on his face, her lack of professional garb didn't offend him. She realized how vulnerable the situation made her. Standing before him almost stripped bare, she saw he still looked at her with a gleam in his eyes.

"Business," he whispered. His hand rose to her face and his index finger stroked her cheek before he pulled his hand back. "And now, personal."

"Join me?" she asked and she signaled for the waiter, hoping to buy a few seconds to gather her wits. Mitch ordered whatever she was drinking and the young man moved away. His drink was brought quickly and left on the small table separating them.

"You look wonderful, Avery," he started, unable to look away from her.

"Thank you." She stared at him, not quite sure what to do with him now that he was here. If she hadn't had the erotic dream just before his appearance she might have been in better control of her bodily wants but with the idea of him still fresh in her mind, she found it hard to think beyond the possibilities. She focused on his hands and then glanced away, his eye catching hers with a cynical smile.

"If you don't have other plans, have supper with me tonight," he ventured. She watched him before answering and he saw the hooded look her eyes took on.

"That's probably not a good idea."

"Do it anyway, Avery. No pressure. Nothing has changed since the last time we met. I understand you're looking for a different type of life style and it's just a meal in a public place." He watched her intently, adding, "Afraid you won't be able to keep your hands off me?" His mock smile jolted directly to her heart.

"Be careful what you wish for."

"Supper and some conversation. You're staying here?"

"Yes."

"Tell me about it over supper; I'll meet you in the lobby at seven."

"Afraid to come and collect me?" Her brown eyes softened with her smile and made him laugh outright.

"Absolutely!"

She settled back in her seat, her decision made. "All right, as long as we both understand nothing has changed." He moved away quickly and she was nervous and relieved at the same time. It was an odd combination. Gathering her possessions, she headed back to her room and napped for an hour before showering and getting ready to meet him.

While she dressed for him, Avery kept repeating to herself that it was just a meal in a public place, not an invitation to his bed. She was annoyed with herself that the second invitation was really what she wanted from him. She'd made her choice and would live with her decision. Only seeing him again made her question the validity of it all.

Why couldn't they just enjoy each other for a night? The answer was simple: she felt too much for him already; his touch would be too much to fight. He'd been honest with her and she with him, right from the start at Jack's. No going back now, no second guessing herself. If she got the Hamilton II job, her future lay in a drastically different direction than Mitch was planning for his.

****

Promptly at seven, she emerged from the elevator and wandered through the opulent lobby. He would have been hard to miss in any crowd, but tonight, in his black suit and grey shirt, he stood out from all the rest. Avery had put her hair up and used little make-up after her day in the sun. The white linen sheath she wore was tailored to her figure, smoothing over her large breasts and nipping at her waist before it hugged her hips to mid-thigh. She'd worn high heeled sandals and no stockings.

Mitch watched her walk directly toward him and held out his hand to her. She hoped he saw her as tanned and stunning, understated yet elegant. He was the man who lit her dreams on fire and made her brain ache with want and desire. "You're stunning," he started, reaching a hand to her.

"Thank you, a little sun always helps. And you, kind sir, look delicious." He held her gaze and it was Avery who finally cracked a smile.

"I can see this is going to be an interesting evening, Avery. Thank you for accepting my offer."

"Where are we going?"

He led her outside the hotel to a waiting town car. As the driver opened the rear door he told her he'd picked a restaurant across town. The restaurant was elegant yet understated. At the sight of Mitch, the host lead them to a corner booth that was quiet and private.

Avery wanted to ask how they knew him but didn't. She settled beside him and looked at her surroundings. The restaurant was elegant yet comfortable, a hard combination to achieve. When she mentioned it to him, he gave her an odd smile.

"Somehow, Mr. Amazed," she started after the waiter poured their wine, "I feel like the proverbial lamb about to be led to the slaughter. Quiet, candlelit room with romantic music..."

"I gave you my word, Avery. I won't push you. But that doesn't mean we can't enjoy a quiet meal in beautiful surroundings." He tipped his glass to hers and watched her as her cheeks heated in the low light. "Why are you in Las Vegas?" he asked, effectively opening the flood gates for her to talk about the project for the Hamilton Hotel.

****

He watched her animated explanation of her design in different terms than she'd used at the meeting earlier and was glad the decision was made before this dinner took place. It had all been a formality, but he'd wanted to see them all in action one more time. "And if you get it, how will it change your life?"

Avery went still and turned away from him. "I suppose besides the financial stability it will allow me to work out here for a few months, enjoy a change of scenery, work with new people. It's all very exciting and scary at the same time."

"You, scared? I'd never have though that."

"Not afraid, just ... new is always a little bit scary until you begin. It's the anticipation factor," she told him and his eyes zeroed in on her full lips.

"What will happen if you don't get it?"

"I go back to New York. Nothing ventured, nothing gained. I got a few days away on someone else's expense account. Met a few people, had an educational time in many ways. And I got to see you again." There was a slight hesitation before she added, "You do turn up in the strangest places."

"You'd be surprised, Avery."

Their meal was served but Mitch hardly tasted it. He found it hard to think about anything except the woman seated next to him. He led her onto the dance floor and held her close through several songs, well aware that he had an audience. He forced himself to keep her at a respectable distance even though it was hard to accomplish.

"Mitch," Avery's eyes went liquid in the minimal light as she looked at him.

"I think I'd better return you to your hotel, Avery."

"Why?"

"Because I'm walking a tight rope here with my promise to you and what I really want to do." His tone was tight and she didn't confront him, although she let her hip graze against his arousal before taking her seat.

He signaled for the check and led her into the cool night air. "I was going to ask if you wanted to take a ride to the dam, the lights are quite spectacular at night, but I'm afraid the time in the car will tempt me beyond my human constraint, Avery."

The car took them back to her hotel and he walked her inside to the elevator. There was no offer of a drink somewhere or a walk down the main boulevard to keep him closer for a while longer.

"I'd ask you to come up, but that's not a good idea."

"No, it's probably not, even though it's what I want. Good luck tomorrow. Can I call you in the evening to see how you made out?"

"Why not let me take you out for supper? You can soothe me if I lost and congratulate me if I win." Her eyes flashed at him and he burst out laughing. She did, too, and moved to touch his cheek, watching him intently the whole time.

"I'd like nothing more, but I'll be gone in the morning."

"Why is it every time we meet you're off the next morning?"

"Bad timing, I suppose, or good, from another perspective."

"I see what you mean, even if I don't like it."

"Good night, Avery," he whispered, his lips just grazing her cheek.

"Good night, Mitch."

****

She watched him walk away quickly and let out an exasperated sigh. Once back in her room she let herself think about him holding her on the dance floor and laughed. She'd been ready to bring him back to her room and take whatever he was willing to offer her. Only his level head kept her from throwing herself at him. She didn't sleep well and the next morning she found she couldn't eat. Not because of the meeting, but because her Mr. Amazed left her at the elevator, just as he promised. She'd been annoyed that he had. Just what did that say about her?

Bob came into the room after an assistant set up the conference call. They were all seated and waited anxiously for the decision. The strong voice that talked to them thanked them all for their time and effort. He went on to say that the suites weren't the only project he was looking at. With that, he offered Ms. San Francisco the job of overseeing the spa areas of the new hotel.

Norman Ethan, Mr. Canada, was offered the main restaurant. Avery drew a deep breath after congratulating Norman. He seemed pleasantly relieved with the offer while Ms. San Francisco wasn't.

Suddenly it was her turn and the voice on the other end of the conference call congratulated her. She'd been offered the high roller project and accepted with more grace than she'd believed her excited self could exude. When the meeting was over, she and Norman went to a celebratory lunch, neither of them having enjoyed their breakfast waiting for the final decision.

****

She'd been given the use of a car and driver and spent most of the afternoon at the site, taking notes and photos. She returned to the pool for a swim late in the day, and then gone back to the site after dark and taken copious notes and more photos of the hotel to work from. Back in her room after nine, with supper from room service, she was packing for her morning flight home when the phone rang.

"Hello?"

"Avery, how did it go?"

"Mitch, I got it. I'm so excited. It's a lot of work, but I'm looking forward to it."

"I'm happy for you," he started, then hesitated. "You understand why I left you last night?"

"Yes, I do. And I'm both thankful and annoyed about it." Her laugh softened her words. "How did your day go?"

"It could have worked out worse. Two out of three things today went well, and the third is questionable."

"Want to discuss it?"

"No, not now. I just wanted to congratulate you."

"But how could you know you weren't going to get a depressed, dismissed designer when you called?"

"I know you; I had faith in your ability."

"Thank you, Mitch. Where are you?"

"On my way to Australia for a few months."

"Oh."

"Yeah, I know, Avery. Before seeing you yesterday I was excited about the project; now I could care less."

"It will be exciting again; you just have to get settled and get to work."

"And you, what happens now?"

"I divide my time between here and New York for the next few months. The projects at home are well on their way to completion and I held off booking anything new until after I found out about this."

"What will you do with your fat commission?" he teased.

"Bank it for my baby," she said immediately, then realized her slip up.

There was a deafening silence on the other end of the phone for several long seconds before she spoke again. "Mitch, I know you're disappointed in me, but it's what I've always wanted. This job will give me the freedom to keep working and be a full-time mother."

"Any candidates in mind, Avery?"

"Yes, one, but he's not willing." She couldn't believe the words flowed so easily from her.

"Or not capable?"

"I'm sorry, Mitch, I didn't mean it like that. It's just that...Damn you, after meeting you, I've decided I'd rather have my children alone than to pick a husband or mate that isn't..."

"Me?"

"Yes. I'd rather be alone and hope one day I will meet another man who makes me feel like you do. I'll take nothing before settling, especially when it's so important. No matter how hard another man tried he'd never be you."

"What will you do?"

"I've done some research. There's an excellent fertility clinic in Manhattan."

"Avery, it sounds like you've thought it all through."

"I have, Mitch, and I've you to thank for it in a strange way."

"Me, how?"

"You told me not to settle and I realized I'm not willing to. But it doesn't mean I still can't have a family. I'm a strong, competent woman. I'm not afraid of doing this alone."

"Your children will be blessed with a wonderful mother, Avery."

"Thank you, Mitch."

"I've got to go. Good luck with the project. Show them what you're made of, and knock them dead."

"Thanks. You, too, and Mitch, I wish things were different."

"So do I, Avery. For the first time in my life, so do I."

He hung up and knew deep inside him it was

the best thing for her life. It was just that he felt like crap in his. The need for her was so strong he couldn't bear it. It was a good thing he really was heading to Australia for a few months. If he had access to her, he'd never let her alone and he knew it.

Rethinking all of his life's decisions was difficult enough, and he knew after weeks of thought that he couldn't change his past, only his future. Not when it came to Avery and the children she wanted. He'd never be able to fix that for her. It was best to let her go and get on with life in the present.

Chapter Six

Avery was exhausted and had never felt so alive. The months she'd worked on the project had been invigorating and the end result stood before her in all its glory. While it had been the hardest job she'd ever done, it was by far the most impressive. Having a budget with seven figures allowed her complete freedom in deciding on her materials.

It was just past nine p.m. and she was taking a last look around at the evening lighting when she felt the presence of a second person. Turning to look behind her, she didn't restrain the gasp that worked through her when she recognized him.

"Mitch?" His name was barely a whisper on her lips. He walked slowly toward her and she couldn't believe he was really there. "What are you doing here?" His hand reached to stroke her cheek and her eyes slid shut at this touch.

"Very impressive, Ms. Lambert. I approve." He glanced down her body, taking in the worn jeans and man-tailored shirt she wore. Her hair was braided down her back. "Can I get a tour?"

Avery had no words for him; her throat had gone dry upon realizing it was really him. She motioned for him to join her as she moved toward the first suite. Opening the door to the north suite, he saw it had turned out as she had anticipated. As if the guest walked into a Swiss chalet combined with an Adirondack log home; the only thing missing was the snow. Rich leathers and suede fabrics prevailed. He glanced into each area and smiled when she stood in the doorway of the bedroom.

The south suite was different, as he knew it would be. Soft pastels mixed with white wicker and rattan with large ceiling fans made you feel like you'd been spirited away to a tropical paradise. The east suite offered an Asian feel, but the west suite was still his favorite. The contemporary air gave a feeling of warmth and comfort, combined with elegance. The materials she'd chosen all worked within their spaces and he smiled at her when she all but marched him from the suite.

"In a hurry to get me away from the bedrooms, Avery? Don't you want to christen one of them?" She laughed aloud at him.

"Yes, that's why we're back out here. Somehow I don't think Mr. Hamilton would appreciate it." She let her index finger trace the line of his bottom lip and his tongue slipped out to taunt her.

"Do you know that for sure?" he teased.

"No. Actually, I've still not met him. Not until tomorrow when he comes to tour the suites."

"Don't worry, he'll love them. They turned out exactly as I pictured." Mitch caught his slip and watched her face drop.

"Like you pictured it?"

"Your descriptions were very detailed. I've imagined the end result for months."

"Oh," she watched him intently, not sure why but she knew something had changed. His body tensed and his face grew tight, an expression she'd never seen on him before. "Mitch..."

"Avery, there's something I need to talk to you about, before tomorrow morning."

"Come back to the hotel with me and I'll buy you a drink," she suggested.

"No, not yet." His hands went to her shoulders from behind and he pulled her to his chest. "Avery, I haven't been completely honest with you." He held her tightly when she started to move away. "Please listen, it's important." She settled under his hold but didn't lean back against his body like she'd been before.

"What is it, Mitch and why are you here now?" They stood looking at the new complex and she felt him take several measured breaths. In the short time he took to compose himself, Avery felt the world as she knew it slipping away.

"I'm very happy with the project, Avery; I knew my decision was right."

"Your decision?" This time she pulled from his hands and swung around to face him, the confusion showed in her body language and her expression. "Mitch, exactly just what are you saying?" She stared him down and didn't blink. Ultimately it was he who looked away.

"Before we met at Jack's the first time, I'd decided you'd get this project from your original concept. Meeting you was just a formality. I never expected to find you…I mean, oh, hell, Avery." He looked away and his defeat sealed his fate.

"Speak very carefully, Mitchell, because what's forming in my mind is going to get you physically hurt!"

He watched her hands ball at her sides as she spoke. He laughed aloud at her and it didn't help. He stilled his nervous smile and stood to his full height, towering only slightly over her.

She stood to her full height, not intimidated by him in the least. "Tell me who you are," she whispered.

"Promise not to hit me?"

"*No!*" Her brown eyes flared at him and he just shook his head.

"Avery, I'm Mitch Hamilton." He stood tall and proud and didn't flinch, waiting while she assimilated the information.

"The owner is Michael Hamilton…"

"Michael M. Hamilton. I've always been Mitch or Mitchell; my father was Michael. It just made life easier around the house not to have two Michael's."

Avery was stunned by his revelation. She took a few steps back from him and stared wide-eyed. "Is that why you never came around the site?"

"Partly. I was in Australia for a while."

"But…"

"Avery, if I'd told you what would have changed? You might not have taken the job or if you did and I stayed around, we would have ultimately grown to hate each other. I wanted you for the project; staying away was the only way I could see to accomplish that."

"You son of a bitch…" she said in an anguished tone then rounded on him so fast he didn't have time to prepare for her.

Her fist slammed into his stomach with more force than most men could muster and while he automatically bent in pain, she gave him a right cross to the chin. It sent his head flying back and his teeth snapping together. Off balance, she staggered backwards a few steps. Only after finding her in his line of vision did he take a breath. She stood staring at him, her left hand cradling her right fist as her eyes filled with tears.

Betrayed and angry didn't begin to describe how she felt. The high of completing the job was gone, dread replacing it. Did everyone know? Was she so oblivious? How stupid a woman was she? The thought that she almost begged him to come to her room the last time they met pushed her over the edge toward anger and she knew she had to let it out. This wasn't the time to work through the problem like a rational being. This time she wanted to lash out at him and make him pay for his betrayal. And she had. While her hand hurt, it was worth it just for the plain, shocked look on his face.

"Avery..."

She heard him but didn't answer, turning away and slowly walking back towards the main portion of the new hotel. He didn't follow her; instead he rubbed his jaw and knew he'd sport a bruise there tomorrow. Deciding to let her go, he moved to his car and drove back to his office. He waited two hours for her to cool down and used the time to ice his face. She had taken him completely by surprise. But it was his fault. He had known how deep her emotions could run. Wasn't that part of the reason he stayed away all this time? Just past eleven, he phoned her room.

"Avery, will you come down and have coffee with me?"

"Are you a glutton for punishment, too?"

"Yes, in some respects. Please, a public place? Anywhere you want, just give me a few minutes to talk to you."

"A public place. The cafeteria down the street; give me twenty minutes." She didn't slam down the receiver, but it wasn't lightly put back in the cradle, either.

Avery knew she'd see him, first to apologize for physically hitting him and second because she wanted some questions answered. She'd manage to get through the walk-through tomorrow and never look back.

****

The fluorescent lighting in the twenty four hour cafeteria was bright, to say the least. He was waiting in a window booth for her when she arrived and spotted him immediately. Other than a red mark near his mouth, he seemed intact. She slipped into the seat across from him and ordered coffee. Neither said a word until they had been served and the waitress moved away.

"Are you hungry?" he started.

"No." He watched as she tried not to look at him,

catching her eye and smiling at her. “I’m sorry. I shouldn’t have hit you. It wasn’t ladylike, to start. Second, it wasn’t called for. I apologize.”

“Accepted and understood. I knew no matter how I told you it would anger you.”

“Anger me; is that what you were afraid of?” She let out a sarcastic laugh and pulled the cup toward her. “Mitch, I have to know. Please don’t lie to me.” He nodded and she continued. “Was anyone aware of our previous meetings?”

“No, only Jack, and he doesn’t have anything to do with the hotel.”

“Bob didn’t know?”

“No. He might have guessed when I didn’t attend the two final meetings, but he never said anything to me and he would know better than to speculate to anyone else.”

“Now I understand why you never gave me a last name. Would Jack have told me if I’d have asked him?”

“Yes, I never asked him to lie, I never mentioned you to him again.”

“Why this whole charade? I don’t understand.” She relaxed back into her seat and stared at him. “It’s important, Mitch. Why?”

He leaned across the table, his hand resting palm up. The last time he had done that she had slipped her hand into his. Tonight, she wanted to do the same thing but held back.

“If you think back carefully, you’ll realize that you’d already sent in your prospectus by the time I met you the first time. I was in New York and wanted to see what you were doing with Jack’s place. I’ve known him for years and know the level of perfection he demands. I wanted to see how you handled him and his project.” He sat back and laughed aloud.

“Damn, Avery, the first time I saw you I knew I wanted you, and not because you were intimidating the builder. There was just something about you that snapped inside me. I knew being around you for a long period of time without wanting you was impossible."

"Why did I get the job?"

"Because I wanted what was best for the hotel and, ultimately, what would be best for me. I knew from the original bid you'd get the job; the rest was just protocol."

"You let the other two designers do all that work for nothing?"

"No, I let them do that work just in case you disappointed me. And when you didn't, I knew I could shift their talents to the other areas." He paused and sipped from his now-cooling coffee. "Avery, bombshell that you are, I wouldn't have given you the project if I wasn't sure you could complete it to my satisfaction. If not, I would have swapped you to the spa or the restaurant."

"What would have happened if I'd slept with you after the house warming?"

"I don't know. Any answer I give you would be speculation. It wouldn't have changed the outcome of the job. You had it before that night, in my mind at least."

"I'm so confused by all this. Did you meet either of the other two?"

"No. I stayed away from all three of you on purpose, to make sure you didn't feel singled out in any way." They quieted while a waitress topped off their cups and moved away. "What happens now, Avery?"

"I don't have a clue!"

"Tomorrow morning, will you still be here to give us the tour?" She only nodded her head yes. "Always the professional," he teased. Her head shot up at him and her eyes narrowed. "All right, wrong choice of words. Avery, we have to move past this."

"No, we don't. In actuality, nothing has

changed." She sighed and stared at him. "Tomorrow, I'll give you and all the other backers the grand tour and slip back to New York. Nothing has really changed except I feel like I've been played. I know it's not rational, but I feel betrayed somehow." Pausing, she tried to reconcile the hurt she was experiencing and couldn't. "It may not be rational but it's accurate."

"I'm sorry. I'd hoped to be able to break it to you in a softer way, but I realized there wasn't any other way. And I didn't want to wait until tomorrow morning with a crowd of spectators, just in case..."

"In case I reacted badly and slugged you?" She finally laughed and he visibly relaxed. It annoyed her that she couldn't stay mad at him even when she wanted to. He'd affected her that way from the start. There was something inherently different about him, about her when she was with him.

"I guess I had that one coming."

"Yeah, I guess so."

"What happens now, Avery? You yourself said nothing has changed. What will you do after tomorrow?"

"Take a few weeks off, then go back to work."

"Did you have a location in mind?"

"Probably the Caribbean. Someplace warm where I can swim, and think."

"I have a lodge at Lake Tahoe. Come away for the week with me?"

Avery was stunned by his invitation, as he knew she would be.

"The way I figure it, a week away won't kill either of us, and you've definitely earned the time off. Helen can run the showroom for another week whether you're in the Caribbean or at the lake with me. Maybe I'll be able to get you out of my system if we finally consummate our relationship. Nothing else is working, Avery. I'm consumed with the thought of you, all the time. It's not how I normally operate, as you're well aware."

"And what if it backfires on us?"

"I don't know. But I feel like if we don't take this time for us, we never will, and our lives will go on. I just don't want to live with the regret of letting you walk away."

"But, Mitch, you know my deepest secret."

"I can't do anything to help you there, Avery. Let me give you a holiday to remember. When you're up late at night feeding the baby, maybe you'll think of me and smile."

"I don't know," she whispered. Staring out the window at the night lights and people on the strip, it all seemed so surreal to her.

"I don't either. Come away with me, no pressure, same rules as before. I won't touch you if you don't want me to."

Avery laughed heartily at that comment. "Mitch, we both know that won't happen."

"A man can hope." He stood and reached for her hand, pausing only to give their waitress a large tip for taking up so much of her space without eating. She gave him a wide smile and told them to come back any time. Outside, he turned to her.

"Think about it. Tomorrow is Tuesday. We could leave in the afternoon. Next Monday I leave for Australia again, and I won't be back for months."

"And I go back to New York. Who else will know we're away together?"

"No one has to know. I'll have the lodge stocked and give the housekeeper the week off."

"I don't know…"

"Don't decide now. Let me know tomorrow after the preview." He kissed her cheek and walked in the opposite direction of her hotel, which was his hotel. Avery went back to her room alone, not sure what to do. Granted, she wanted to jump at the chance to be with him, but what would happen when their time was over? Could she go back and not ever see him again?

****

The preview was a success; all the parties involved showered her with compliments. Mitch, too, but in an unobtrusive way. While she had been with the group all morning, she hadn't heard a single person dare to ask him about the red mark on his chin. In fact, she decided several times that it might be divine justice if she asked him, just to see how he'd answer, but she hadn't.

She noticed him hanging toward the back of the group, milling on the fringes, talking on his cell phone often. By noon it was over. All that remained was for her to pack her bags and decide whether she would fly back home or take the week at the lodge he'd offered.

Chapter Seven

She slipped away from the reception with ease after accepting a final round of congratulations from the group of backers. Her telephone was ringing as she opened her hotel room door. There was no need to rush; she knew it would be Mitch and he'd let it ring until she answered it, knowing she'd just left the lunch. Avery took one long, deep breath and let it out before grabbing the receiver.

"Yes?"

"Well done, Avery."

"Thank you, Mr. Hamilton."

"What have you decided?" There was a long pause and neither of them spoke. Finally, she cleared her throat, her voice almost a whisper of words floating across the air to him.

"If I come, no pressure and nobody else will ever have to know?"

"Yes."

"Are you sure there's enough room?" she tried, hoping to have a graceful retreat from her want.

"The lodge is huge, six bedrooms in the main house and three smaller homes around the compound. Avery, we're adults. You know exactly what I'm offering you, a week away with possibilities that end next Monday. I want to be with you, Avery, but it's just for this time. You understand that, don't you?"

"Yes, just a week away, our private retreat

before reality begins on Monday."

"Yes. Am I canceling your flight back to New York?"

"Yes. I'll be packed and ready within the hour."

Ultimately, there was no decision to be made. She didn't want to pass up her one chance to be with him, to experience him on a private and personal level. She rationalized that once they were together she'd gain perspective and be able to get on with the rest of her life, a life that didn't include him.

"Good, I'll send a bellman for your luggage at one." He hesitated only slightly before adding, "Avery, I'm really glad I was your choice."

"I hope you still think that way next week, Mitch."

"I will, and so will you. I promise. Just some time to relax and unwind."

She laughed into the receiver at his parting words as she hung up. Since she was already packed, she used the time to figure out just when and where she'd lost her mind. Accepting his proposal sounded so logical, when she knew deep down they'd both hurt to some degree by next week.

The idea of being alone with him, even in a huge house, didn't ease her mind. It was her choice and she was an adult. She wanted this time with Mitch. Just for herself and her memories. Hopefully it would remain their private time and the world would be none the wiser.

Downstairs at the registration desk, she checked out and arranged to have several cartons of her supplies shipped directly back to her New York showroom. Mitch met her just as she was finishing the details. Placing his hand on the small of her back, he smiled to the man behind the counter and directed her toward the entrance where his driver was waiting.

****

Avery awoke with the most wonderful dream

fading from her memory. She was flushed from the attentions Mitch had been lavishing on her naked body from her dream. But she found reality in his warmth pressed against her, his lips at her neck, tracing a line of kisses along her collar bone. She stretched under him, shifting to accept more of his body along hers while she came wide awake.

His arms caught and stilled her until she was fully aware of where they were. A smile crossed her lips and her hands came up to direct his mouth towards hers. Mitch pressed his lips against hers, sucking first her bottom lip then the top lip into his mouth, teasing them with his teeth. He allowed the tip of his tongue to taste the warmth of her, exploring and learning her, until she found herself moving under his weight, trying to reposition him.

"How was your nap?" he asked, pulling her to an upright position against him.

"I can't believe I fell asleep; must have been the wine with lunch," she told him in a dreamy voice.

"That will teach me to take a business call when we're in flight," he teased.

"Yes, it will." She stretched again, this time letting the sleep fade from her completely. "How much longer?" she asked, focusing on his face.

"We'll be landing in half an hour," he started, as her hand moved his from her shoulder to her breast, the size of her overflowing what even his large hand could hold. He groaned against her and finally pulled back after teasing her nipple to fullness with his touch.

"Here and now, Avery, or do we wait until we get to the lodge?" His eyes took on a look she'd only seen in the office at Jack's apartment. He was giving her the choice and she knew she'd wait for more time.

"The lodge, but," letting her hands drop along his chest, she found him through the wool of his pants and shaped her palm to cup him. Mitch swelled against her hand and let his eyes drop closed. "Oh, Mitch, what are we gonna do?" She asked, her lips to his throat, her free hand unbuttoning the collar of his shirt. Her tongue darted against him and he shifted against her.

"Avery, keep this up and we won't have to wait for an answer to that."

"All right," she sighed, but didn't move her hand or her lips. Her assault continued, working him into a frenzied lust. He came alive under her touch and she wanted more, needed more from him before she allowed herself to believe they were really together, that it was real between them and he wasn't a leftover of her dream.

As if understanding her, he pressed her back against the leather sofa as his hands roamed her upper body, skimming over her breasts and down her rib cage. His lips went to hers again in a kiss that made her instantly slick and ready for him. Mitch let one hand wander down her thigh and back up to her junction only to feel her heat penetrating the clothes she wore.

"Oh, Avery, you really are literally hot. Let me taste you."

She groaned when his fingers left her and moved to her belt. Only the cabin bell made him still against her. The male voice told them they were circling over the airport and would land within the next ten minutes. Mitch let his head drop to her chest and she laughed as she ran her fingers through the long, dark, silky strands.

"The lodge," he started, and she laughed.

"The lodge," she told him, but didn't pull away from his hands.

They waited until the plane was banking on its final approach before he let her up. She struggled to right her clothing and smooth back her hair. "How far away are we?"

"About a forty-minute drive," he told her as he

stood and shifted inside his suit pants. "And it will be a long forty minutes, unless you want me to tell them to take us back up for an hour?"

"I'll take the lodge," she told him and took out her mirror to check her appearance. Pulled together by the time they landed, they walked to his SUV, parked near the private air strip waiting for them. Their luggage was loaded with minimal fuss and they were on their way. Mitch drove after handing her a map. He pointed to where they were and where the lodge was and told her about the area and small towns they passed through.

Turning off a main road, he drove for several miles before he slowed and pulled off his seat belt to navigate the rest of the road. At the crest of the driveway she saw a small, A-frame house and wondered.

He read her mind as he told her it was Irene and Lewis' home, the caretakers. They lived there year-round. Irene was responsible for the interior of all four homes on the site and Lewis kept the outside in order, winter and summer. They were retired teachers and the situation worked for them both.

Irene had taught home economics at the high school level and Lewis had been a landscaper by trade before finishing his degree in the evenings. He'd gone on to teach at the agricultural college for twenty-five years. This position gave them great flexibility of time yet required them to use their skills. It seemed to be a situation that worked out for all of them.

The second house he passed was what he called the guest house. It had four bedrooms and baths and he used it for business associates on occasion. The third was another small A-frame, only it was closer to the main compound. This was his mother's home when she chose to use it. From there Avery could see the pond he and Jack had teased about and beyond that the main house.

Mitch parked near the front door and let her wander around while he unloaded the SUV. He found her around the back of the house, staring down at the lake below them.

"It's magnificent, Mitch. I'd never guessed it could be this beautiful."

"You should see it in a few weeks, when winter comes. It's spectacular, Avery."

"Is this your main home?"

"Mostly. Come, I'll show you inside."

She took his hand willingly and was led into the lower level of his home. There was a recreation area, pool table, and bar area, a huge television and sitting area in front of it. There were video game machines in the corners and several smaller tables for games. There was also a full bath and changing area that led through to the glass-enclosed swimming pool. The year-round pool sparkled with the light reflected from the setting sun.

The second story was made up of the kitchen, living, and dining areas. The far corner was a den, with another large television and stereo area centered there. The third level housed four bedrooms and baths and his private office.

The fourth floor was the master suite. A huge sitting room fronted the largest master bedroom Avery had ever seen. The custom bed sat on a platform in the center of the room, catching light from the floor-to-ceiling windows. A seating area was in front of the stone fireplace which was set and ready to be lit. Through a dual dressing area were the two master baths, his and hers. There was another smaller room; Avery figured it to be about fourteen foot by fourteen foot. It was decorated as a small sitting room but she thought it would function as a nursery with only minor changes.

Mitch waited by the window, watching the lake below them as she wandered around the room. "Where should I put your bags?" he asked, letting her make the decision on her own. His voice gave away the tension he was holding.

For the first time, Avery realized he was nervous. It was a pleasant thought, she realized, knowing she wasn't the only one still apprehensive.

"I'll spend a night in each room until I decide," she teased, watching with delight as his jaw dropped slightly.

She laughed at him and didn't resist moving closer to him. "Are we alone?" Her hands went to his shoulders, sliding around the back of his head, just before angling his mouth toward her.

"Yes, Irene and Lewis won't bother us. They won't come past their driveway unless I call them for something."

His eyes told her he wouldn't call them and she knew her decision had been made months before. Without hesitation, she moved away from him, pausing only to pull off her blazer and drop it on the back of a chair.

He watched from his position as she wandered around the room once more before going to the large bed and stripping off the pillows that lay above the comforter and tossing them onto the floor. The comforter came next. Then she started to unbutton her shirt. Her slow striptease mesmerized him as she moved around his bedroom without a second thought. Her boots and slacks came next. Standing before him in just a lace bra and panties, she moved toward the bathroom.

"I'm heading to the shower. Join me," she told him and didn't wait to see if he'd follow.

She made herself comfortable in his master bath, adjusting the multiple shower heads for temperature before stripping off the last of her clothes. The spray cleansed her body and reawakened her need for him. The soap was taken from her hand seconds later and his replaced hers against her body. The lather slid over her wet skin as his hands traced along her. She turned in his arms and pulled him to her, his excitement presenting itself for her. With the dip of her hand she cradled him, learning him with each caress.

Avery turned him under the spray and dropped to her knees in front of him, taking the length presented to her. As she stroked and toyed with him, he sighed under her movements. He groaned when she tasted him and let out a growl as she engulfed him in her warm mouth. For long minutes she continued to manipulate him until she felt his legs tremble. Forcing herself to pull away, she rose and rinsed her hair under the spray. "Mitch?"

He pushed his body away from the shower wall and dragged her from the cubical, pausing only to pull a plush towel around her body while he used a second to blot the water from her hair, then picked her up and carried her into the main room.

Darkness had started to settle around them during their shower, setting a natural stage for them to explore each other. Following her down on the bed, he moved over her, his lips to hers until she felt him throb against her.

"Mitch, please, come inside me," she groaned.

"Later. There are other things I want to do first," he whispered, but she pulled away from him. Leaving his bed wasn't what he expected of her and he rose to question her. Only when she returned with several packages of protection from her purse did he relax.

"Later for the rest. I've waited almost a year to know how you'd feel inside me; I want you now, Mitchell."

Her look told him this wasn't the time to assert his authority, especially when her lips had taken him again, her hands working his length at the same time. Avery pushed him back on the bed and continued to love him, only stopping when he whispered her name.

She rose above him, protected them and let her weight slowly drop over him; her body swallowed him in minute increments until he was buried inside her. It was an exquisite exercise in tortured pleasure; her excitement welcomed his invasion, reveling in the delicious stretching of her body and mind.

Gone was the instinct to suck in her stomach to look slimmer; instead her mind gave her body permission to take everything Mitch had to offer freely, without restraint. For one short week alone in the woods with him, she would be her true self. Avery wanted the memory to be accurate in details, good and bad. Being honest with herself and him was her true road to freedom.

"Damn, Avery, you test my control," he started.

"Mitch, I'm so full," she managed, before dropping to his chest and searching for his mouth with hers. His tongue tangled and mated with hers, each thrust echoed by her hips.

Avery felt it building inside her, knew she had to have the release she'd dreamed about for so long. She pushed away from his lips and sat back up, taking him deeper. Her eyes slipped closed as she used her weight to center him inside her and to push her over the edge into the abyss he'd created with his first kiss.

Avery felt him throb once more and let herself fall; his grunt and one last thrust sent him catapulting with her. Dropping onto his chest once again, she felt his hands steadying her as she relaxed. Dragging her damp hair from her face, he shifted her, only to deepen his position within her. Avery hid her smile against his chest and used her inner muscles to work with him, surprising them both when she was rewarded with a second release and Mitch's growing attentions. He slipped her under him and took the position she'd dreamed of, pushing into her moist heat with a rhythm that beat in the back of her mind whenever she allowed herself to think of him.

Lying under him, she knew he'd never love another woman the way he loved her. She was open and honest with him, accepting and experimental, solid in his arms. A groan worked its way up his chest as his hand reached to cup her breasts, his fingers playing with her erect nipples with the same rhythm as his hips. Avery let her eyes slip closed and her mouth drop into a perfect oval of invitation.

His movements became hurried and intense and he watched her face as she followed him for a second time that day, from the intense darkness into the shattering pin point lights that danced on her eyelids. Her hands gripped his waist and pulled him tighter and she felt him lose control. He managed to drop beside her, taking her with him as he rolled off her. Still inside her, they laid on their sides, her head tucked against his chest, her hand making a lazy pattern on his stomach with her nails as they relaxed.

"Mitch?"

"Hum?"

"You are amazing. Do it again!" she teased, only they both knew she wasn't really teasing. He propped his head up on one hand and stroked her with his other.

"Now or after food?"

"Both," she whispered as her teeth ran along his chest, finding his flat nipple and teasing it to fullness under her tongue.

"Oh, Avery..."

****

It was hours later when they finally stumbled into the kitchen for sustenance beyond what their bodies could offer. They maneuvered with ease around each other in the large space, both content to listen to the evening news as they prepared their snack. The late night comedian was finishing his monologue as they finished eating. With just the light from the television flickering in the background, Mitch moved behind Avery, pressing her against the counter. His hand pulled her hair from her neck and his lips found a new patch of exposed skin to explore.

"Avery, somehow I got the impression you wanted candlelight and romance?"

"Sometimes I do," she whispered. "Tonight, I just wanted you. I've thought about you since that first kiss in Jack's apartment."

Palming an envelope from his pocket, he slipped his arm around her waist and pulled her up against his growing erection, dropping the toweling robe he wore before his fingers pressed her against him.

"What do you want, Avery? Tell me what you pictured all those months?" His fingers dipped lower, her silk robe falling open with a quick tug of the belt. He instinctively found her spot and she let her head drop back on his shoulder, thrusting her hips towards his waiting hand. He stroked her absently while he whispered that he'd dreamed of taking her right here, over the counter.

First his index finger slipped inside her, drawing out her moisture. He throbbed against her back and she flamed inside, contracting around his finger as soon as he replaced it. Mitch still had her hair in his other hand, and used it to push her down over the counter.

He pulled the shoulders of her robe back, exposing and effectively trapping her arms. His mouth to her ear; he sent a chill down her spine as he moved the cloth from between them and pressed his hardness at her entrance. She gasped and shifted over him, accepting his invasion, sucking it into her deeper as she ground back against him.

"God, Avery," he managed, just before he drew back from her and grabbed her waist, holding her while he thrust into her. She matched each of his movements, letting him set the pace, accepting the domination he craved, just as he'd let her drop onto him earlier. Avery went slick around him and knew he felt it, his teeth on her neck told her she was right and they both doubled their efforts.

"Avery, you're so tight," he said, dropping his hand to graze against her. One light touch and he sent her into orbit, following along without control, down with her as she collapsed onto the cool surface. For a long time he stilled above her, his fingers still lightly caressing her.

"Thank you," he whispered, before forcing himself to stand behind her, taking his weight from her and ultimately disengaging from inside her. She balanced her weight on her hands for a moment and he pulled her robe back up over her shoulders before turning her into the circle of his arms. With her head on his shoulder, he lifted her up to sit on the counter, his chest supporting her.

"Damn, Avery, never before," he said, his lips to her forehead.

"I know, Mitch. I was afraid of this."

"Don't be afraid of me, ever. I won't hurt you, not knowingly."

"I know you wouldn't. But I knew you'd be intense."

"You make me intense." He pulled back to look at her before adding, "And crazed and horny and ultimately sated like never before."

"Thank you." The kiss they shared wasn't teasing, it was agitated and filled with the words neither of them had the courage to say. Avery took out her frustrations against his tongue and lips, willing him to understand just how much he moved her.

The tone had been set for their week away that first night. There was no hesitation to touch or kiss, to stop and fondle or appreciate. They teased each other and loved each other more. Their efforts were rewarded with a release of tension and longing that made the air thick between them at times. Avery was glad when he would slip away for an hour or two in the early afternoons to handle business.

It left her time to remember who she was and to reinforce to herself that this wasn't permanent. Just a moment in time where reality didn't exist for them. Monday would come soon enough, she decided, and until then, she'd take whatever Mitch could offer her and hope he understand that she never before had loved so deeply and thoroughly.

Her body tanned from the time she spent lazing by the pool; her all-over color excited him each night as he rubbed lotion on her back and shoulders. He'd become obsessed with her breasts, asking her not to wear a bra around the house. It was an easy request, and after two days, when they dressed to head into town, the wire and material felt strangely confining after its absence.

****

Mitch teased her that she'd have to go braless from then on but changed his mind quickly when he realized other men would be watching her. He was shocked by the thread of jealousy that laced through him when he caught a stranger watching her from a distance. His arm went protectively to her waist and the other man moved away with a nod. It didn't make him feel any better, until she turned and smiled at him. Somehow it took the weight from his thoughts and he relaxed beside her.

"Get your act together, Hamilton," he silently admonished himself when he was able to think clearly. He'd offered Avery a simple week of relaxation and he'd make sure his feelings, all so new to him, didn't spill over to complicate either of their lives. Thinking it was easier than living it; every hour they spent together he fell deeper in love with her.

He watched from a distance as she spent time

outdoors sketching the lake and the mountains. It was becoming unnatural for her to be out of his sight. Mitch made a conscious decision to get them out of the house again on Friday, taking her to a romantic supper at the finest restaurant in the area. She sparkled beside him, turning heads as they walked through the crowded space, her long legs exposed beneath the hem of her black dress.

With her hair up, her skin tanned, and such high heels, they made an extremely handsome couple. On the dance floor, it was all he could do to control the impulse to drag her against him, cradling his erection against her. Somehow she seemed to read his mind, her sigh close to his ear. Avery pulled him closer and slipped her arms up around his neck.

"Mitch, it was a lovely supper and the restaurant has a great view, but would you do me a favor?"

His fingers stroked her back, their heat making her press closer to him. "Anything," he told her.

"Take me home, Mitch, take me home to bed."

He pulled back slightly from her and caught the smile she favored him with, both erotic and playful. They didn't wait until the song ended; rather she took his hand and led them back to their table. Avery waited until they were on his private road before releasing her seat belt and sliding towards him, her hand cupping him.

"Avery?"

"Mitch, you drive me crazy at times, you know that, don't you?" she told him before slipping her hand tighter around him.

He slowed the vehicle and coasted toward the lodge, letting her fingers message her intentions. They never made it technically into the house; instead, she moved through the lower level, stripping as she walked. She dropped her coat over the back of the sofa along with her purse. She paused at the bar while he opened a bottle of wine and slipped off her shoes. Her hair came down next, the pins dropped onto the bar's glossy surface.

Taking the glass he offered, she turned her back to him, lifting her hair out of the way before asking him to unzip her. As her dress fell loose around her shoulders, she let it drop to the floor, stepping out of it as she moved into the pool house. Following close behind her, Mitch stopped to turn on the underwater pool lights as he followed her lead, stripping along the way.

He sat at the end of a lounge chair to slip off his shoes and watched her drop her bra poolside. Her hand rose to her lips and she tasted the wine, only to put it aside as she drew down the silk panties covering her. In another step, she was gliding under the water away from him.

His thought that she was going away from him struck him hard and he fumbled with his zipper in his haste to join her. The only hesitation he made was to put their glasses and the bottle of wine closer to the edge of the pool before diving in to join her.

Avery waited in the deep end for him, treading water to stay afloat. When he surfaced beside her, it was easy to wrap her body around him, capturing her mouth in a kiss that told her what he wanted. The water supported their weight and they floated together with him embedded deeply in her.

"Damn, Avery..."

"I know, Mitch. Just love me, my Mr. Amazed," and he did, to the best of his ability, long into the night. Eventually they made it to the bedroom but not before most of the wine was gone and they'd explored both the pool and the hot tub.

Chapter Eight

Michael Mitchell Hamilton woke the next morning alone and the feeling literally sickened him. He forced himself to stay in bed for a few minutes and control his breathing. When she wasn't in the bath, he headed downstairs, figuring she'd be in the kitchen. That, too, was empty. He spotted her out by the pond, dressed in jeans and a bulky sweater. Her large frame was folded over her knees that were drawn up to her chest. Her hair blew in the light breeze and Mitch's heart contracted.

He'd known he was in love with her but the reality of letting her go was suddenly the farthest thing from his conscious mind. He pictured her with him, all the time, traveling with him, being his alone. Forcing himself, he made coffee and dressed, quietly joining her, carrying two mugs, the steam visible in the early morning light.

"Thanks," she said, accepting his offering.

He folded his long legs to the ground beside her, watching the pond as she did, hoping for the right words. "I woke up alone and didn't like it, Avery."

"I woke up next to you and realized I liked it."

"What do we do?" He waited for her answer and wasn't surprised when she told him the truth.

"You were right, Mitch, that night at Jack's. You said ultimately most women still want a family. The thing is..."

"Is what?" He held her look, needing to see her

expression.

"I know you don't want any part of me after Monday and I can accept that; it's just that I didn't think I'd become so attached to you in such a short time. I can't help wondering what it would have been like for us if we worked it out." He stilled beside her and she laughed aloud at him. "Michael Mitchell Hamilton, I wish you could see the look on your face right now. You'd think I told you I was an axe murderer. Relax; I know reality comes back on Monday."

"What do you wish, Avery?"

"That I could have it all, everything I ever dreamed of, including you, Mitch. I know you don't want children and what they bring and I do. That hasn't changed. I just wonder if you're not shortchanging yourself by not exploring if you could love a child just because and not have it's parentage be utmost in your mind."

"If I could do it for anybody, I'd do it for you."

They looked at each other for a long time before she finally spoke. "Thank you. But we both know it's not what you want and what I've wanted for so long." They fell silent, watching the sunrise over the pond and below them the lake. "So, now that I've gotten past my bit of melancholy, what do you have planned for us today?" She smiled at him over the top of her mug and didn't turn away when he reached to run his fingers through her hair.

"Avery, if I could..."

"No, don't make promises you have no intention of keeping. I'm not asking you to change, just telling you what I was thinking about. I knew when I accepted your invitation I'd become attached, and I still came. I wanted this time with you, just for myself." Her finger pressed against his lip to silence him. "You forgot who you were dealing with; don't ask a question if you don't want an answer."

"Avery, I've fallen in love with you and I know I

have to let you go." There was a strange hitch in his voice, a vulnerability he'd not heard before.

"I know, Mitch; I've loved you since Jack's party. It doesn't make it any easier to admit it. We'll both go our separate ways in a few days. So we have two days left, let's make the most of them." She stood and reached for his hand. "You asked me earlier in the week what I dreamed about you doing to me. Let's take a walk through the woods and see what kind of trouble we can get into!"

She winked at him and sprinted toward the house, collecting their jackets before he could change her mind. He met her in the living room, stopping her before she could run from him a second time. His arms went around her, stilling her motions.

"Relax; I've got a surprise for you today. Be ready to leave in half an hour." He reluctantly moved away from her and headed toward the kitchen. Avery watched him take several bottles of water from the refrigerator before turning back to her.

When she was about to ask, there was a commotion outside the lodge. "Time's up. Ready to go?"

"Well that was fast! Where are we going?" she whispered, her voice husky with want and they both knew what she wanted.

Taking his outstretched hand, she followed him outside to watch him greet and then introduce her to the man unloading the horses from his trailer. They were saddled and ready to ride a ridiculously short time later. She met Lewis, the property's caretaker and the horse trainer, before they took off into the wooded acreage of his land.

After half an hour, he told her they'd just left his acreage and were on the state park land that bordered his property on two sides. The sun rose hot in the sky and Avery stopped to pull off her down vest. At the top of the next rise the lake unfolded below like a mural painted just for them. The beauty of the land and the lake took her emotions by surprise and she didn't stop the few tears that ran down her cheeks. Stopping his horse beside her, he leaned forward but didn't mention her tears.

"This is why I come here, Avery. It's the closest I can get to God and his creations. I feel at peace here."

"I can understand that. It's stunning, Mitch."

"Avery, I've never brought a woman here before," he started.

She smiled at him before throwing her head back and laughing at him. "Nobody willing to ride into the mountains with you?" she teased.

"No, I mean I don't bring women to the lodge, ever."

"Oh," was all she managed to utter when she realized what he was saying. Somehow the intensity between them charged the air around them and she moved her horse closer to him. "Mitch, there has to be a place where we can…"

He watched her blush and his laugh relaxed his tense body. "Take the trail to the right, Avery."

She followed his directions and ten minutes later they came to a clearing. The small plateau was hidden amongst the trees, a private retreat with a small waterfall tracing down the rock wall to their left.

"This is one of my favorite places on the land," he told her as he dropped off his horse and walked him to the water. He dropped the reins on a low tree branch and guided her horse next to his. Large fingers supported her waist as he helped her down, letting her body slide along the length of his. Stretching, she watched him move into the trees and return with a large wicker basket and blanket. Her eyebrow went up in a curious question and he didn't hesitate to answer.

"I had Lewis drive around and leave us lunch."

That was all she got by way of explanation and didn't push for more. She helped him spread the blanket and dropped beside him, exploring the contents of their prepared lunch, suddenly aware they'd skipped breakfast. Avery spread out the food while Mitch opened the wine.

The light breeze cooled the sun's hot rays against their skin and Avery stripped off her heavy sweater, her nipples budding in the temperature difference. The thin T-shirt she wore without her bra let him know she was thinking along the same lines he was. His hand reached to stroke her through the cloth and her warmth spread through him. It didn't take any conversation; she simply pulled the shirt over her head, baring herself to him. His groan told her she was on the right track as she moved closer to him.

"God, Avery, you're more beautiful than the land," he started, but didn't finish when his lips became attached to her. Lying sated beside her after an afternoon of loving in the open field, his fingers traced the line of her waist down her belly and along her hip.

"I wish I could watch your body change when you're pregnant. Your breasts will swell and your nipples will..." his lips didn't hesitate to bring her peak to tighter fullness. Stroking between her hip bones, he laid his head against her. "I would love to watch your body swell with my child, Avery," he told her in a whispered voice that had them all too serious and they both knew it.

"You'd probably turn out to be the kind of man that couldn't look at a woman after watching her give birth," she started, then sobered. "I'm sorry, that was rude and uncalled for."

"Yes, but it's easier to be defensive than think about what might have been."

"I suppose," she started. "Mitch, can I tell you something?"

He pulled away and moved beside her, his head supported by his hand.

"I'm scared spitless sometimes when I think about being a single mother, yet I can't let it go. I know deep down this is right."

"You'll be a wonderful mother, Avery. I see it in all the little things you do every day." He hesitated and finally asked what he really wanted to know. "Are you sure you're not jumping ahead? Maybe your Mr. Right is out there somewhere and you just haven't met him yet. Maybe you don't have to do this alone." He shifted to stroke her again and watched her melt under his hand.

"No, I've looked and I don't think it's meant to be perfect for me. Maybe that's part of my test in this life. To have my children and love them enough for two parents."

"Avery..."

She shifted onto her side and put her finger to his lips. "Don't. I might say yes and then where would you be?"

She stood and stretched in the afternoon light, not conscious of being naked in the field. Instead, she seemed to be at home in nature. While her back was to him, he studied her long legs and full, tight butt. She slimmed at the waist and her brown hair glistened with red and gold highlights from the sun. Shifting his erection, he fought the urge to go to her.

He constrained himself to be content with watching her, his hand unconsciously stroking his length. When she turned back to him he realized the visual she took in.

Seeing him there, lying on his side, his head propped with one hand, his other stroking his hardened length, Avery let out a gasp. She moved beside him and watched him pull his hand away.

"Don't stop," she whispered, as she dropped behind him, her hands on his shoulder and belly as she watched him stroke himself. "God, Mitch, you're beautiful, do you know that?" Her lips moved to his earlobe and she continued to tell him what he did to her, how he made her feel as she nibbled at his neck and chin. When he would stop so would she.

"Avery?"

"Let me watch you, Mitch," was all she said as she shifted him to rest his back against her chest, her long legs stretched out on either side of him. Her fingers continued to knead his chest and arms, occasionally stopping to tease his nipples. Her breasts cradled his head and he continued his movements.

"Mitch, do you have any idea how erotic a sight you are? All solid male stroking yourself? It's making me hot, Mitch. Finish for me," she whispered as she talked against his ear.

A groan worked its way up his chest and out his throat and his hand moved faster against himself in a motion that only he could understand. Watching intently, she knew when his body tensed and she watched him climax. Her fingers pinched his nipples and her mouth was sucking his neck between her lips. She left a red mark that would later turn purple. All that mattered was the experience they shared. His hand fell to the side and she used her fingers to draw his essence towards her lips to taste.

After several trips her finger drew his moisture along his bottom lip and she shifted to take it against her own. He growled against her and shifted her under him. His fingers danced over her, finding her wet and ready, hot and waiting for him. He pushed her back on the blanket and moved her hand to her junction, pressing her fingers to herself.

Avery closed her eyes and accepted what he wanted. With slow, deliberate movements, she used her fingers to complete the action just as he had; only this time his lips were on her breasts, his hands lifting their weight towards his waiting tongue. He lay beside her and watched, pushing his hand over hers when she'd stop to enjoy his tongue bath.

"If you stop, I stop," the teasing tone allowing her to groan as she let her finger dip inside herself. In a motion that only she could understand she let her release overtake her.

Mitch felt her quake against him and drew her hand to his lips, sucking her fingers deep inside to taste her release. Avery crumpled against his chest, exhausted and sated.

"Rest for a while," he whispered as he moved her hair from her cheek. "I love you, Avery. No matter what, that will never change." His hands on her steadied her before she could move to look at him and his head dropped on top of hers.

For a long time they stayed that way, locked against each other with his words floating through the mountain air. He refused to let maudlin thoughts, however accurate, spoil the short time they had left.

It was a long time later when he finally shifted behind her, taking her hand to his lips.

"We should get dressed; it's a long ride back," he said and she allowed him to pull from behind her. They managed to get dressed with minimal conversation, and, strangely enough, it wasn't uncomfortable. He'd simply been honest with her, and she with him. Maybe if it was awkward, it might have been easier to toss aside the emotion that they both felt during the lazy ride back to the lodge.

****

Sunday it rained, black clouds blocking any chance the sun would have to skim through the darkness. It was a day conducive to staying in bed and they did, venturing out only for food and showers. Miraculously, by Lewis, she assumed, the Sunday newspapers were waiting for them when they reluctantly rose for coffee, and they took both items back to the bed with them. Reading, dozing, and loving took up the rest of their day and it wasn't until later that night, while they grilled steaks for their supper, that reality came knocking.

"Would you like to go to Australia for a few weeks? I can't cancel this trip but you could come with me?"

Her arms circled him from behind and she only sighed against his back.

"I wish I could, but reality comes back tomorrow. I have to get back."

"Will you go directly to the clinic?" he asked, his words not malicious, just curious.

"I'll wait until my next period, then set up my appointments."

"Avery, beyond healthy, would you rather a boy or a girl?"

"Either, both," she said, laughing aloud. "I suppose both have their merits, but a girl would be easier without a husband, no bathroom problems in public places. I can't take a boy into the women's room for too long and..."

"Call me and I'll come back to help," he told her.

She laughed at him as she set the table. "Yes, I can see it now. Your cell phone will ring and I'll be on the other end asking you to fly across the country because my son needs to use a public restroom and I'm uncomfortable sending him in alone at such a young age!"

"You have thought this all through; I didn't really think you had."

"This is a life altering decision, Mitch, not something to be taken on impulse. I've waited five years to do this. I'm in good shape and I'm healthy. I'm also thirty-two and my time is starting to narrow."

"Avery, if I could get past the genetics and be with you, I think I could."

"Don't, Mitch, don't even think it. I told you yesterday, I might say yes and then where would you be? Stuck with a wife and family that you never wanted…no."

"People change," he started and stopped when he saw her face.

"I'm serious. Until I met you, I never would have considered the idea, but you make me believe we could make it work."

"Mitch, I love you, I have since Jack's, probably before. But I know deep down this is the last thing you want for your life. You're free and easy, you don't want the baggage of a family to tie you down, and it's not how you operate. You'd lose your edge."

"What if I choose to?"

"You'd eventually hate me for it; somewhere along the line you'd feel cheated and claustrophobic."

"Then travel with me; we'll take the baby, get a tutor when he's old enough to be in school."

"You've decided I'm going to have son?" she teased, trying to lighten the intensity their conversation had turned to.

"If you have a daughter you won't need me for bathroom breaks," he countered.

"Mitch, one of the things that drew me to you is your ability to know yourself, to understand what it takes to get you through the day. At Jack's, you told me hands down, no family or ties, it would change you. And you were right, for you." She stood back and looked at him, seriously appraising him. "If we hadn't met, you'd still feel that way. I can't be the catapult to life changes you never wanted." The exasperation in her voice started to slip through.

"Let's just change the subject. Reality comes back to haunt us both tomorrow. For the rest of tonight, let's just be us, Mitch, please?"

His hand circled her waist and he drew her to him. "No matter what, I'll still love you." His head rested against her forehead and he paused before adding, "And it scares the hell out of me."

"Me, too. But this time with you, it's been like a gift, something to carry with me, a memory to relive when times get tense."

He pulled the unfinished steaks off the grill and turned off the gas.

"You read my mind. Forget about food for now." She drew his mouth to hers and took his hand to her breast. "Mitch, love me so I won't forget," she said, her voice breaking just before tears slid down her cheeks.

He didn't acknowledge them, just swung her up in his arms and carried her to the floor before the fire in the living room, taking her away from reality and their words, to the place where they connected with groans and whispered words of want and need.

Avery understood Mitch completed her in many ways, she just hoped she'd still be complete on her own after experiencing how he loved her. Trying to get a grip, she reasoned to herself it was because they would part that they were both able to let go and enjoy each other.

****

He'd asked her if she would see him when he got back and she'd said no. They'd discussed it on the ride to the airport earlier that day and they both knew extended contact would only hurt them in the long run.

"I think it's best if we enjoyed the memory of us, Mitch. Anything else and it would hurt too much. If we run into each other, I'd rather know my presence won't make you uncomfortable. I'd never want that to happen."

"That couldn't happen," he told her, but as he glanced at her quickly he realized it was one of her fears. "No matter what, Avery, if you need me, for anything, please don't hesitate to call me. I'm dead serious about this, and even though you're pushing me away for self-preservation right now, I need you to understand that I'm not just placating you. If for any reason you need me for anything, please tell me you'll call."

She gave him a glancing nod but no verbal reply. He laughed at her before adding, "At least file it away for future reference."

"Okay, I can live with that," she finally told him with a smile.

When they'd arrived at the airport and he'd seen she was checked in, his kiss let her know that their time together hadn't been a mistake. He held her close to him and only when they announced her flight did he pull back from her, pressing one last kiss to her forehead before heading her toward the security check in.

"Travel safe, Mitch," she'd whispered, not looking back after clearing security. He pulled his sunglasses from his pocket and hid his watery eyes from the public around him.

****

Lying in her own bed for the first time in weeks, she settled into the space that was once so comfortable and reassuring to her. With time, she'd make it feel that way again, for now she just had to get through the nights alone. Days moved easily for her, work taking her mind away from the memories.

****

Mitch paced the conference room and wondered what he was doing there. The thrill of the game was gone, all his thoughts centered on Avery. She tried to let him go with grace and he understood how hard it was for her to leave him at the airport last Monday and take her separate flight back to the east coast and the life she'd built there. It was his mind that had her wrapped around him, her arms and legs holding her to him and it was in his mind that he realized and finally acknowledged two things. First, she was the best thing that ever happened to him in his life and, second, she was gone from it for more reasons than he could overcome.

He'd thought long and hard about loving another man's child and came to the conclusion that it really didn't matter in the end. The child would be part of Avery and he would accept him or her because he loved the mother. Gone were the cavalier statements that he'd used so often to dismiss his paternal feelings. Gone was the front he put forth for the world, never pausing to watch a family together or to peek at the baby in a stroller or carriage. Gone was the time when the sound of a child's cry turned him cold. Now he heard need in a baby's cry and wanted to sooth it, and he heard happiness in a child's laugh and ultimately knew it would never be because of his actions that a child laughed with delight. And he'd never hear Avery laugh again.

Forcing himself, he pushed back to work, making the deal count, making the game foremost in his mind. It sounded good to him when he was alone with his thoughts; following through was harder. He set a new pace for himself and didn't relent even when his body told him to rest. Mitch pushed harder and faster then ever before and still the end results didn't impress him. The material things he was so proud of didn't matter anymore, the figures on his bank balances didn't impress him either. When he looked at the numbers, he saw only black and white, no grey or color as he always did with Avery.

The sound of her name could make him harden at the most inopportune moments. He stayed away from Manhattan on purpose; knowing the impulse to contact her would be too overpowering. He'd never thought of himself as a weak man; now he knew how foolish he'd been. Avery Lambert was the only thing that mattered in his world and he'd sent her away forever with pat answers and reckless statements designed to do just that: keep her or any other woman at a distance.

His mind made up, he'd returned to ask Avery to marry him, only to have his fantasies destroyed by an outside influence. He'd spent too many hours thinking about the time he'd lost with Avery because of Alexandra. Time he'd never get back. It made his resolve to protect the future more intense.

Chapter Nine

Avery stood before her bedroom mirror, thankful her pregnancy in the new century allowed her to wear clothes that announced to the world her pending motherhood. If she'd been relegated to wearing tented tops with bold stripes or T-shirts that had an arrow pointing down with the word "Baby" printed over it she would have enjoyed the whole process much less.

Tonight, thanks to a few designers who understood a woman's pregnant body should be appreciated, she stood in a burgundy dress of silk jersey. It hugged her figure and didn't hide her slight belly. If anything, the cut enhanced her bustline and prompted the eye to take in her status. Her hair was down and curled around her shoulders, her make-up light. She knew she looked great, but she wanted to knock Mitch Hamilton off his feet, even if she was larger than ever before.

He'd told her once he would like to see the changes in her body while she was pregnant. Well, here was his chance. How strong was he at heart, she wondered? Having always been a large woman, she felt big next to most people. Now with the baby on board she was getting larger than even she could have imagined. Would her weight send him running for the hill of non-pregnant women?

She also understood that it was a test; could he really appreciate her condition or was it all bravado talking when he didn't have a chance in hell of having to really deal with her or her changing body? Either way, the answer would present itself in a short time. Checking the bedside clock, she saw she had only minutes before he'd be at her doorstep. When he was, she'd have a few choice words for him and his ideas. Standing tall and taking one last look at herself, Avery glared at the mirror.

"How dare he think I'd be his proxy wife!"

She was coming down the stairs as her bell rang and she didn't hesitate to pull open the door to confront him, her words on the tip of her tongue. It wasn't until she took one look at him in his navy suit and light blue shirt that the words locked in her throat.

On impulse, she moved to him, her hand reaching to his cheek as he dipped down to kiss her. Just a slight brush of his lips against hers and her sigh fell forward, sealing her fate. His strong hands moved around her back and pulled her to him for the kiss she'd dreamed about for months. Long and slow, he explored her with his lips and tongue, renewing their connection, forcing them both to journey back to the beginning, before reality came between them. It made her resolve to protect the future more intense. Stepping back from him, Avery had to pull back her smile and force her eyes to narrow.

"You bastard!" she whispered, calling him the rude name for more reasons than she could sort out at the moment. She followed it up with several sentences in Italian that he didn't need an interpreter for. For kissing her the way he did, for looking the way he did, for making her melt in his arms with just his touch, and for the stupid proxy stunt. She held onto that one and gathered her anger at him.

Mitch was prepared for her. "Yes, but at least it got you to see me." His words were a flat statement. "You never would have seen me without some kind of stunt and we both know it. All I want is some time to talk with you."

"You did this on purpose, over a long holiday weekend, so I wouldn't be able to get help until you had your say." Her words were a similar flat statement, letting him know she understood his game.

"You wanted time. I'll give you some time. But it won't change the ultimate outcome. I won't marry you, Mitch, under any circumstances. And if for any reason this stupid idea of yours turns out to be legal, know this, you'll pay for all of it to be absolved."

He nodded his head in acceptance and she shook her head at him.

"Where?" she asked, her tone terse and confrontational.

"Where what, Avery?" He moved into the living room behind her, his hands in his pockets. "Where are we going for supper or where would I like to talk?" When she didn't turn to him, he moved behind her, letting his lips lower close to her ear, adding, "Or where are we going to make love?" She tensed before him but he didn't stop. "I'll give you some time to absorb the idea, Avery, but you will ultimately be my wife and we will raise our son together. Get used to me being around. That's not a threat, it's a promise."

He straightened and pulled back, openly appraising her. "You look stunning, Avery. You make me hard with just a glance."

"Thank you." So now she knew his intent, except she didn't know how much strength and longevity his statement carried. She wondered if he knew himself, knew his limit.

"I want to touch you, to explore you, Avery, but we need to settle a few things first. Important things, so I suggest we leave here and have supper and talk…"

"Mitch, I'm not going to fall back into bed with

you, especially after this stupid stunt," she said, finally turning around to meet his eyes. With a rueful smile she knew his puppy look would be the end of her sanity. "I need to stay mad at you, can't you understand that? It's all I've got right now. Please, if you want to talk to me, you have to keep your distance physically from me."

"Avery, I'm not trying to harm you or our child."

Her eyes flashed at him and he finally smiled. It was a warm and kind smile, one she wanted to seal away and keep forever. He watched her before asking her if she was ready to go. They had to go someplace where they could talk openly and honestly.

****

When she was settled in the Italian restaurant, the low light, background music and corner booth set her nerves on edge. He'd behaved like a perfect gentleman so far, only taking her hand to help her in and out of the car. He ordered red wine while she drank sparkling water. Their order placed, she sat back and appraised him.

"You look tired," she started, drawing a resigned breath. "Where would you like to begin?"

Mitch turned toward her in the booth, his arm rising along the back. It would have been so easy to shift towards him and be enveloped against him. Resisting the urge, she straightened in her seat. "How did you feel when you got the test results?" A dose of reality would act as a cold shower to them both.

"Probably about the same as you, numb. I couldn't believe it, wouldn't let myself believe it, because if it was a mistake I don't think I could have stood the letdown. You talk about staying mad at me to keep me at a distance; I left you with the hope of a child on one hand and holding an agreement to relinquish all my rights to that child in the other. I stayed mad at you for that, Avery. That's how I got through those days. Only after the second test…"

"Second test. You really thought I'd try and trap you?"

"I didn't know what to think, only that until I had proof I couldn't believe." He drank from his glass, dipping his finger in the wine and drawing it across her lips. "Taste familiar?" he whispered, watching as her tongue followed the same path as his finger.

"The hot tub," she murmured, and drank from her water to dissolve the taste and the memory.

"I'm sorry I doubted you, Avery, but I had no other choice. However, since then I've done a lot of thinking and soul searching. And there are a few things you need to know." He pushed back in his seat while their pasta was served, using the food as a diversion to the words he spoke.

"I said I felt numb when I found out I wasn't sterile. What did you feel when you realized you were pregnant?"

Avery tossed her head back and laughed at him, and her tense attitude fell away. She told him how she'd thrown herself into work when she returned to New York and didn't think about it until she had a few queasy mornings. That sent her to a calendar and, ultimately, the realization.

"I understand numb, Mitch, on several levels." She pushed her pasta dish to the side and he raised his brow at her half-eaten plate. "I'll take it with me and have it around midnight when my blood sugar drops, all right? I'm taking care of myself and my…our …baby. I eat in small portions all day long, I feel better that way. End of subject." He nodded and accepted the fact that he couldn't walk in and second guess her.

"Keeps your insulin leveled that way."

"Yes, and I feel better. You've been doing some quick research."

"No, not quick. I've been reading for the last

three months, Avery, getting ready to come back to you."

"But?"

"Later, we'll talk about my coming back when I did; for now let's just put the pieces together."

"Okay. I was numb because the dates matched and there'd only been you. I was numb when I realized I was actually pregnant, three home tests later. And I was so dumbfounded that it happened, I couldn't believe our luck, my luck. I didn't relish the procedure to produce a child on my own, Mitch. The old fashioned way was much better." She smiled and watched him carefully.

"And I was ultimately numb when I knew I couldn't keep the baby from you."

He lifted his glass at her, a sincere smile on his lips. "Avery, if you had, and I found out later, I don't know what I would have done."

"It doesn't matter; I didn't try to hide from you. I knew that would be wrong for us."

"And one of the first things we're going to do together is take care of the person who did try and keep us apart. Are you free the next few days? I'd like you to come to Atlantic City with me to handle Alexandra. My mother will be there and she's looking forward to meeting you."

Avery's mouth literally fell open and her hand moved to her belly. "Grandmother," she whispered, but Mitch heard her, his arm coming around her shoulders and pulling her toward him. She didn't pull away; instead she leaned into his shoulder and said, "Thank you." Letting him hold her was as much for him as it was for her, she decided, but forced herself to pull away.

****

"Why do you want me there to handle Alexandra?" They both waited while their entrees were served and the waiter moved away. "Surely you can't expect me to confront her?"

"Actually, I want both of us to confront her together, with my mother as back up. I want her to understand how wrong her decisions were and that I won't allow her to destroy my wife and family. She's been a friend of the family for years; our fathers were in the same law firm. She's always just been around. But she overstepped her bounds here and it's time she realized her future lies in a different direction."

"And your mother?"

"She's known Alex all her life and her presence will make her understand they'll be no second chances or jockeying for position. She's being released and sent on her way with full family support. I won't allow her to stay near us and risk her interfering ever again. I don't trust her with you, the baby, or me. End of subject. How's the chicken?" he asked, watching her dig into the lightly breaded filet along with the wilted greens tossed with olive oil.

"And just so you know, it was technically my mother's idea to get married and work it all out later on." Mitch watched her face drop with that bomb and laughed.

"What are you talking about?" Sampling the salad, she tasted more while waiting for an answer. "Mitch?"

"She said I should take you to Las Vegas and marry you before you had a chance to think. Somehow I didn't think getting you on a plane would happen, at least not with you conscious and I wouldn't take a chance with you or the baby by slipping you a sedative."

Avery tried to give him a harsh look but softened, knowing he'd never hurt her. "I think I should have a long talk with her after all."

"Well, be kind, she was just so excited. But then it did trigger the proxy angle when I saw an old movie on television."

"Remind me to thank her," she countered with a smile. "Mitch, what did she say when you told her?" Avery looked down and refolded the napkin on her lap.

"She was as stunned as I was, but when it sank in, she was happier than I've seen her since before my father passed. She got that twinkle of life back in her eyes, Avery, that look of bewilderment. She suddenly looked younger to me, alive again, renewed." He reached for her hand and drew it to his lips. "Thank you for that."

He set her hand down but didn't pull his away. "Her name is Ruth and she's gonna love you."

"What about our situation. Was she upset by that?"

"Mom learned to roll with the punches a long time ago. Whatever we decide to do will be all right with her as long as she gets to spend some time with you and the baby."

Avery literally squirmed in her seat next to him and he squeezed her hand. As if he could read her mind, he added, "We'll figure out how to blend our lives. It will all work out, I promise. I'm a very flexible man when it comes to my wife and family."

"Family, yes; wife, no."

"We'll see."

"Damn you, Mitchell, you annoy the hell out of me sometimes," she started and realized it was the reaction he was hoping for.

"You have to understand that I had this all planned out before you ever entered my life. I was supposed to do this by myself, prepared for it. And you never wanted any part of a wife or child." Pushing her plate aside, she drew a deep breath and told him she wanted to know what was for dessert.

They lingered over a second cup of decaffeinated coffee and Avery smiled at Mitch.

"I've wanted to say 'I told you so,' ever since you walked out of my house, but now it's not as satisfying as I would have thought."

"You earned it. I was wrong."

"Mitch, could we get out of here?" He signaled for the check while Avery freshened up.

Outside in the cool winter air, he seemed surprised when she wanted to walk. He gave his driver instructions along with Avery's doggy bag and pulled her close to his body for the walk back to her apartment.

"Avery, I'd understand it if you felt I was taking over. I mean, you had your plans and so did I. But now that we're gonna have our child, I need for you to start to see me as a partner and parent, and not an adversary that stepped in at the last moment to take charge. I'm asking you to revise your future to include me in our child's life."

"I know that, Mitch. It's all so crazy. All I've ever wanted was a man who would love me and want to have a home and family with me and that's exactly what you're offering. And I'm turning it down at every pass. I can't explain it just yet, so could we just let that side of it go for a while. I'm comfortable with you having access to our child and helping to raise her."

"Him."

"Whatever," she said exasperatedly. "But please don't push me to marry you. Not for a while. Let's just see how the future works out for a while. Can you handle that?"

"It's not my first choice at all, but under the circumstances, I'll allow you some breathing room."

"And the proxy nonsense?"

"We'll put that aside for the time being."

"Aside or annulled?"

"Avery, have you thought about names?"

****

Her apartment was warm and inviting and she asked him if he wanted coffee. Following her to the kitchen, he held his hand over hers when she went to fill the pot.

"No coffee tonight, Avery. I'm not sure how much longer I can keep from touching you and you've been a good sport up until now."

"A good sport, is that what I am?" Her annoyance started to surface and Mitch dropped his mouth over hers, showing her what he was feeling. When he finished thoroughly ravishing her mouth, she wound up pressed against the length of his body, his erection reinforcing his slipping resistance. Mitch let one hand trace up her side and cup her breast, his palm taking the weight of her as his fingers tempted her nipple to life.

"Do I stay or am I going back to the hotel? You decide Avery, but if I stay here, it's not for coffee."

She looked at him and knew he was right. If he stayed, he'd wind up in her bed and inside her. "We shouldn't," she started.

"Not until we take care of business. Can you come to the shore for the weekend?"

"I suppose so."

"I'll pick you up around nine tomorrow morning. Pack enough to get you through Tuesday unless you need to be back Monday night."

"No, but I've got appointments on Wednesday I can't miss." He walked toward her front door with an odd look on his face. "What is it, Mitch?"

"I missed the first doctor's appointment."

"And the second and third. Nothing we can do about them."

"Tomorrow we'll handle Alexandra and spend a few days relaxing. The hotel has a heated pool, so bring a suit."

"Maybe you should handle this on your own or with your mother. I'm not sure my being there will make it any easier for her."

"I'm not trying to make it easy for Alex; I'm trying to set our future straight so we start from a place of trust and comfort." Mitch drew her close,

"I've lost too much time with you already," he told her and turned to leave quickly, only to meet his driver at the door with Avery's doggie bag. Turning he handed her the snack and gave her one long smoldering look. His lips started to curl into a smile and she shook her head at him. He left with the smile still on his lips.

Avery wasn't quite sure what to think but she knew two things: she'd go with him to be a united front when talking with Alexandra, and she did want to talk to Ruth Hamilton. There were no nerves or second thoughts about going. Mitch would have known that. He'd expect her to stand up for their child and he knew the minute they were close to each other, keeping their distance would be an exercise in futility. Never had a man made her so crazy in all her life and if she didn't stop smiling, she'd hate herself.

Chapter Ten

"You're early," she told him the next morning as she pulled open the door at eight-thirty. He was a sight in worn denim and a leather jacket. Her hair was still damp and she hadn't pulled on clothes yet.

"I was anxious," he told her as he took a step back to look at her wrapped in a dark blue silk robe, a robe similar to the one he'd pulled from her body at the lodge. Only now her belly rode below the belt and he didn't resist the urge to cup his hand against her. Avery closed her eyes for just a second and realized where this might lead.

"Good, you can carry my bag down when I'm ready. There's juice and coffee in the kitchen, and I need fifteen minutes."

She moved up the stairs quickly, away from his touch, deliberately dressing before she finished her hair. It was only a few minutes later, when she shut off the dryer, that she heard noise from the room next door. Avery smoothed the front of the longer tunic she'd pulled on. It was comfortable and hugged her curves. She liked the way it made her feel sexy and stylish over long slim slacks of the same material.

Standing in the doorway to the bedroom next to hers, she watched as Mitch went from wall to wall openly tracing the paint on the walls with his finger. While it was mostly in the first stages, the mural continued around the room. It started in the far corner with a mountain and lake in the background and continued. Trees, plants, and animals were sketched in, waiting for their layers of paint to give them texture and life. What she hadn't been prepared for were Mitchell's eyes, glassy with tears when he turned around. He didn't hold them back, only turned away from her.

"It's going to be beautiful, a room any child would prosper in."

"Thank you, that means a lot." Her voice cracked with emotion she couldn't draw back.

"Think you could reproduce it in a few other locations? That way no matter what home we're in, he'll always feel secure in his space."

"What other homes, Mitch?" Straightening, she stilled at his words.

"The lodge for one. The small sitting room off the master bedroom is a perfect place for a nursery. I keep suites at each hotel in Atlantic City and Las Vegas that are always at our disposal." He'd been able to get his emotions in order and turned back to her. Seeing the look on her face made him laugh. "Too much too soon, Avery? We'll talk about homes later. Let's take care of first things first and the first step is..."

"Is what?" she asked, trying to diffuse the heat between them with an attitude of indifference. It would have worked if he didn't look at her with his soft brown eyes.

"You look beautiful in dark green," he said and moved closer to her as his eyes took in the soft slim pants that matched the longer top, its neckline in soft waves just above the hint of her cleavage. It hugged her curves in a tantalizing way and he wanted to touch her.

"No matter what we decide, I'd be honored if you'd wear this, Avery, if only to symbolize our personal understanding." He slipped open the velvet box and pulled a platinum band from the black satin bed it rested on. Three diamonds stared up at her, glittering in the early morning light of the nursery. "An eternity ring, for our past, our present, and our future." He slipped it on her left third finger and it fit as if it had been made exclusively for her.

Avery didn't try not to look at the ring. "I'm not pushing marriage, just our understanding that we'll raise our child together, and that there will never be another woman for me, ever."

"Mitch…"

"Please, Avery, wear my ring. It's important to me."

"I don't need diamonds to remind me of my feelings for you, Mitch," she said, her voice accepting before she finished.

"No, but I need the reinforcement to the outside world that you're not available." They watched each other intently for several long seconds before she finally spoke. Her mind was running full tilt trying to figure him out as the corners of his lips started to tip upwards.

"As long as it doesn't lead to marriage," she started but didn't finish. She pulled him to her and slipped her arms around his neck, hiding the broad smile on her face. His hands warmed her back and she knew it felt right, was meant to be, even with the strange way circumstances that brought them together.

"I'm ready if you are," she continued, wiping a stray tear from her cheek.

"Afraid we won't get on the road?" he teased as he watched her walk from the room, following behind her to take her bag. He was surprised when he saw a large wrapped parcel lying on her bed beside her bag.

"That goes too," she said, with no hint to what was inside or why she was bringing it along. "I'll meet you downstairs; I want to shut off the coffee pot." Avery left him with his thoughts and slipped past him in the doorway, allowing her hand to linger on his arm for just a second before she forced herself to move away, the words she wanted to say stuck in her throat.

Instead she let her mind wander to what he might look like stretched out on her king size bed, naked and sated. The instant moistening tingle flowed through her and she smiled again, but forced herself to concentrate on closing up the house.

Settled in the SUV beside him, Avery teased Mitch, asking if he had a similar truck at every house and he told her he did. Their drive was a reasonably leisurely one considering it was a holiday weekend and they were heading to the Jersey shore like most of the other travelers on the New Jersey turnpike that morning. He made several stops for Avery to get out and stretch and walk a bit. She accepted his offer to keep her comfortable through the long ride and teased him a second time that his research had been intensive.

As they were nearing the shore, the traffic thickened and Avery knew she had to clear the air before they arrived in Atlantic City.

"Can we talk while you drive?" she asked.

"Of course."

"The ring is beautiful, Mitch, I love it. I'll wear it proudly because it means a commitment to me, too. It means there won't be another man in my life, unless it's this one," she said, her hand dropping to her stomach. "And we both know after my week with you at the lodge, there never could be."

"I was miserable in Australia those months. I wanted to call and ask you to come and I knew I couldn't."

"The thing is, Mitch, and hear me out before you turn my words around, all right?" She waited while he grunted a yes. "I was so prepared to have this child on my own, been preparing for her for years now. And all that time I was preparing for a solo act.

It's not that I don't want your input with the baby, just that I never expected to have a man who wanted to be a part of us. I'm still not sure you really understand what it takes, what the changes will be in your life if you seriously want to be involved as much as you think you do right now."

"I've thought it through, Avery. I'm ready for changes to my lifestyle, as long as they include you and the baby."

"Mitch, I've a very possessive nature, toward this baby and ultimately towards you, right or wrong."

"I wouldn't have it any other way. I expect you to be possessive and careful with my son, and with me." He paused while he changed lanes. "You have no idea how it makes me feel to watch another man look at you. I've never been jealous before, Avery, never. Even at the lake when we were out in public, I secretly sent out daggers to any male I caught looking at you."

Mitch pulled the truck off the road and into the far end of a shopping center and shut it off. He released his seat belt and turned to her, his hands drawing her chin towards him.

"Avery, I had your ring made in Australia. I knew then I'd come back and ask you to marry me, to share your babies with me, months ago. I've been carrying it with me all this time. I had it with me when I found you in the market. I came to Manhattan to ask you to spend your life with me. So let's just drop the concept of me wanting you only since I've learned about the baby." He kissed her lips hard and pulled back. "End of subject." Pulling his seat belt back in place and starting the vehicle, he entered the mounting traffic while she sat speechless.

Avery asked him to pull into a large discount drug store before they arrived at the hotel. He gave her a questioning look and she only smiled at him before slipping from the vehicle. "I'll be right back," she whispered, her hand not resisting the urge to stroke his cheek.

"I'll park and meet you inside."

"No, I won't be long, just wait." Somehow it seemed important, so he just nodded his consent.

"Avery, we don't need condoms this weekend," he started to tease her and watched her face turn beet red. He wasn't sure just why she blushed but he knew now wasn't the time to inquire. He'd have plenty of time to find out later, once they were settled at the hotel and he'd taken care of Alexandra. True to her word, she was back beside him much sooner than he thought possible, tucking a brown bag into the leather tote she brought with her.

"I'm ready," she told him with a smile but with no hint of what her purchase was. They arrived closer to the center of town and he finally started telling her about the hotel.

"It was the first one I bought, eight years ago. It's starting to look a little worn; maybe you can figure out how to give her a facelift without too much disturbance to the casinos and the lobby area. I'd planned on waiting another two or three years before doing any major reconstruction."

"I was here last year, just after the initial letters went out. The lobby just needs some sprucing up," she told him with a smile.

"Then you know there's a more private entrance we could use, but for today, I want to use the front entrance. It's important that the staff get to know you and give you the proper respect…"

"Mitch, what are you trying to tell me?"

Maybe he'd gone too far but it was too late to change the situation. Suddenly this didn't seem like such a good idea.

"I'm asking you not to fight with me in public, Avery, especially in front of the staff. When we're settled in the suite you can holler all you want, just not now, please?"

It was one of the few times his voice had the sound of pleading with her and she just gave him a suspicious look. Whatever questions she might have asked were shut down when he pulled up under the canopy of the front entrance of the Hamilton Hotel, Atlantic City. Their doors were opened and she accepted the hand of a uniformed doorman to help her out.

"Mr. Hamilton, good to have you back, sir."

"Good to be back, Miles."

She glanced toward him and watched him stretch his long frame after the tiring drive.

"I'd like you to meet my wife, Avery Lambert Hamilton," he said, catching her eye over the top of the vehicle and winking at her.

"A pleasure, Mrs. Hamilton, welcome." She accepted his handshake and refrained from glaring at Mitch. "Your suite is ready and your mother arrived a few minutes ago. I believe she's gone up to her rooms."

"That's fine; we'll give her some time to settle in." Mitch was at her side, his firm hand on her back, guiding her through the lobby. They were met halfway to the elevators by Hank Waters, the general manager. He was older than Mitch by a good twenty-five years, graying at the temples, with glasses in aviator frames. They shared a bear hug and Avery was introduced as his wife.

"Welcome, Mrs. Hamilton," Hank started, kind blue eyes meeting hers.

"Please, call me Avery," she said, accepting his handshake.

"Your suite is ready," he said as he walked with them to the elevators. "I've taken care of the details you requested last night."

Once in the small moving box, Avery steadied herself on Mitch's arm when it jolted into movement. She listened to the small talk about the hotel and was shown into a beautiful guest suite, a bellman following behind with their bags. She watched as he automatically put their things in what she assumed would be the master bedroom. She moved to the window, pulling back the curtain.

"Thank you for not slugging me in public," he teased, as his lips grazed the side of her throat. "I've ordered lunch; it will be here in twenty minutes. Do you want to rest for a while or," he pulled back when she twisted in his arms.

"What?"

"Mitchell, you exasperate me to no end, do you know that? Do you do it on purpose?" Her hands stilled against his chest but she didn't move away.

"Of course I do, but you love me anyway," he said, his eyes never leaving hers. It was a stand-off they accepted.

Avery let her head drop onto his shoulder and his arms swiftly came around her, holding her close.

"Better hug me now while you still can," she started, only to be interrupted by a knock on their door.

"That will be either the food or my mother."

"I'll freshen up and be right back." She'd been right when she said she needed him to keep his distance. Every time he held her it only reinforced his wants and needs. He knew the whole situation was starting to wear on her.

****

Avery stood in the marble master bath and tried to get ahold of herself. She brushed her hair and reapplied her lipstick and felt human again. Now if she could just get her emotions in control and stop thinking about getting him naked and in a bed. Ever since he left her last week, her mind had been overrun with images of them together. Only now, in his hotel, she wondered what his reaction would truly be to the changes in her body. Best to find out now, she decided, before she got too attached and he realized he couldn't or wouldn't want to follow through on his original plans.

Entering the living area, she immediately saw the resemblance. Ruth Hamilton was as tall as Avery, her hair a soft bob of grey-white silky curls. Her eyes were the same chocolate brown as Mitch's, only the shape of their faces was different. There was no need to announce her arrival. Mitch pulled away from his mother as soon as she entered, as if he could feel her presence.

"Mom, this is Avery Lambert," he started, but was all but pushed aside as Ruth strode purposefully toward her.

"Avery, I'm so happy to meet you, come and sit down so we can get acquainted." She took Ruth's extended hand and allowed her to lead them to the sitting area. "Mitch, I could use some coffee and I'm sure Avery probably wants something to hold her over until supper."

"All ready ordered, Mother," he said, not accepting the dismissal in her tone. Avery laughed at them both.

"I'm fine, Mrs. Hamilton, really. And you're right, I am hungry. As to dismissing your son so we can talk, I doubt that will happen right now." Both the Hamilton's turned to look at her.

"Mitch, I approve already."

"Thank you so much," he started, only to be interrupted by room service and their food.

****

Two hours later, Mitch interrupted the marathon of conversation that spanned Avery's childhood and career and some of Mitchell's less inspiring moments as a child.

It was an odd place for him to be; his mother and his wife, talking as if they'd known each other for years. His child, growing inside the beautiful woman whom he'd fallen in love with and thought he'd never have. The reality of it all overtook him once again and he held back the wave of emotion that passed over him.

"Enough, she'll be running from the hotel in tears if you don't stop now, Mom."

"Actually, I'd like to go for a walk if you two don't mind. After being in the car for so long, I'm stiff. Anyone care to join me?" She turned toward his mother and Ruth stood, accepting her offer.

"Avery, don't wander too far on the boardwalk."

Both women burst out laughing at him. He looked stricken and they laughed harder.

"She's pregnant, not stupid, Mitch," his mother snapped. "And she's managed just fine up until now, so take off your leash and let the woman breathe." Having said her piece, Ruth moved to the door. Avery laughed at him, but did pause to drop a light kiss on his lips as she passed by him. His hand went to her arm and held her in place a second longer, his eyes searching hers.

"We'll be fine. I just want to stretch."

"And probably berate me in private for my stupid idea setting off your insane idea of the proxy marriage." Ruth stood tall and Avery laughed again, moving to the older woman's side.

"That's one topic I'd like to cover," she admitted as Mitch watched the two women disappear from the suite.

During the hour they were gone, he paced the room endless times and kept a vigil from the balcony, not relaxing until they were in sight of the hotel. He moved inside and opened his laptop, pretending to be engrossed in whatever was on the screen when they returned.

"Returned safe and sound," Ruth announced as she entered the suite behind Avery. "I'll leave you two to relax. Would you like to have supper alone?"

"No, please join us; I have lots more questions about Mitchell's more awkward moments."

He groaned aloud and Ruth excused herself to

rest.

"We'll meet you downstairs at eight," he called after her. She raised her hand in acknowledgement as she left them alone.

Avery moved to his side and closed the cover of the computer. "We saw you watching for us," she whispered. "I'm going to lie down for an hour. Wake me so I have time to shower?" She didn't wait for an answer, but moved toward the master bedroom and let her body drop onto the huge mattress, sleep taking her almost immediately.

****

Avery awoke in the darkness, Mitch leaning over her, his fingers stroking her arm. "Hi," he whispered. "It's almost seven-thirty. Want to go back to sleep or have supper?" She turned toward him and stretched, pulling him down to her. She let herself bask in his warmth before finally struggling to wake up.

"I need a quick shower and then food. I'll be ready by eight," she told him. Mitch helped her from the bed but didn't hover in the room. She realized he'd already showered and was beside her in a navy blue signature hotel bath robe. He smelled clean and fresh and all male. She didn't think twice when she saw that he was in the bath when she stepped from the shower, his face still half covered with shaving cream. They moved with practiced ease around each other, the feeling a holdover from their time at the lodge.

Avery pulled on a beige wrap dress that accented her hair and eye color. With a few minutes more, her make-up was finished and her hair brushed down her back in long waves. Mitch pulled on a dark grey suit jacket and she paused to straighten his collar, her lips not missing the opportunity to graze against his.

"You are an extremely handsome man, Mr. Hamilton."

"And you, Mrs. Hamilton, were beautiful the first time I saw you in overall's intimidating a contractor. Now, you're beyond stunning." He waited but she didn't explode when he called her Mrs. Hamilton.

"Mitch, we'll talk later."

He took her hand and held it to his lips, his eyes never leaving hers. "I like calling you Mrs. Hamilton, so get used to it. If you want to use Lambert-Hamilton for business I don't have a problem with it. But you are my wife, Avery."

"No fairy tale wedding with all the trimmings?"

"If you want one, yes, but it doesn't change the fact that we are married."

"Only in Australia, I think?" He didn't offer any further information and she didn't feel the need to push. "I'm hungry and your mother will be waiting."

"Let her wait," he told her, his lips taking hers in an intense kiss before he finally pulled away.

****

Supper turned out to be a comical affair with Ruth letting small glimpses of her son's past filter through the conversation. "I suppose he didn't tell you how when he was twelve he decided he'd teach himself to drive because his father and I told him he was too young?" It was said with a mother's love and humor and a little shake of her head. "Be warned, you're going to have to keep a sharp eye on this little one."

"I'll expect help, Ruth. You won't desert me in my time of need?"

"Of course not. Besides, you're going to want some time alone after the baby is born if I'm ever going to get any more grandchildren."

"Let's just get this one delivered before we plan any more."

"I'd rather plan them all," Mitch added, "but I'll wait for a better time to push that subject." Avery let his words hang in the air waiting for her response.

When she didn't comment he visibly relaxed.

Ruth excused herself to her room for the night, but Avery asked her to come back to the suite with them instead. Mitch raised an eyebrow but didn't verbalize his thought. He probably figured Avery didn't want to be alone with him just yet. He was taken aback when her real purpose was revealed.

Back in their suite, she moved to the bedroom, and upon returning she commandeered his laptop. Setting it on the dining table, she invited Ruth to sit down in front of the screen when she had it ready.

"Mitch, meet your baby," she started, her hand reaching to him.

With one hand in his, she touched Ruth's shoulder after hitting the key that brought the baby's first sonogram to the screen. It ran three minutes and basically was a black and white blur of minute movement. She pointed towards a hand and a foot, outlined the baby's head and spine for them and then took a step back, watching the two heads vie for position before the screen. Mitch didn't drop her hand, only squeezed it tighter and dropped his other hand to his mother's shoulder.

"Avery, this is wonderful," Ruth said.

"Amazing what technology can do these days. At first I thought they'd just print out a still picture, but they handed me the disc on the way out and I was thrilled. There's a copy for you, too, Ruth, for your bragging rights. Mitch mentioned you were computer savvy before he was when we were up at the lodge last fall."

"Thank you, Avery. I'll treasure this and definitely use it for bragging rights. Thank you for thinking of me."

"You're welcome. Now one important question, are you going to be a grandmother or Nana?"

"I haven't decided yet. Probably Nana; it sounds younger." With that said Ruth gave Avery a hug and excused herself for the night, promising to return tomorrow morning at ten for their meeting with Alexandra.

Mitch was still in front of the screen after Ruth had long gone and Avery had undressed. She freshened up and pulled on a slip of blue silk over her expanding form. It cupped her larger breasts and skimmed over her growing belly. With her face scrubbed and her hair brushed back, she finally went back to find Mitch, still entranced by the image on his computer.

"It will be there tomorrow, Mitch. Come to bed," she told him. Her words filtered through his mind and he shut down the machine. Staring at her, he didn't move from the chair. "Yes, I said come to bed." She left him confused and delighted as she sauntered back to the bedroom.

Mitch sat beside her on the large bed as he watched her settle against the pillows. "Are you coming to bed or are you going out?" Her fingers ran along his shirt front and he closed his eyes. "Mitch, what's wrong?"

He stood and walked away, pulling the cloth from his chest. Avery heard the shower run and a short time later he was back beside her, wrapped only in a large towel tucked at his waist. He watched her and she realized he was deciding something, just what she wasn't sure.

"Avery, if you'd rather I sleep in the other room for a while…"

"I'd mind very much if you did," she whispered, her hand reaching toward him. "Mitch, it's all so crazed. I know I'm the one keeping you at a distance, but please don't leave me alone tonight." She watched a small smile form on his lips. He dropped his towel and moved beside her, taking her against him.

"I missed this," he told her in a hushed tone. "Every night since we left the lodge I've missed having you beside me at night. Hell, it's no fun having a bed to myself and nobody to fight over the covers with."

"I don't hog the covers," she teased as she let her fingers trace his rib cage. Glancing up she saw the look, one eyebrow raised and a smile. "I don't. I simply want all of them." Her hand dipped lower and cupped him. "And I want to feel you inside me again, Mitch. I've felt so empty, if you can imagine that in my condition."

"Oh, Avery."

"Tell me something, honestly."

"What?"

"Was the sonogram a mistake? Did it make this all too real for you? If I'm pushing, I'll try to pull back, but I didn't want to be holding back."

Mitch covered her words with his lips and kissed her deeply. His hands brushed against her shoulders and pulled her across his lap, settling her against his chest.

"Avery, the sonogram was wonderful. I'm just still amazed that I actually had anything to do with it."

"That's just it; maybe you want more time to adjust."

"I'm adjusted. I'll tell you a secret, but it stays between us, all right?" He took her hand in his and brought it to his lips. "The first thing I did after I got the test results was start a college fund."

She didn't pull away, only sighed at his words. Finally, she laughed aloud and pulled from his grasp. Walking to the window, she pulled back the curtain and watched the boardwalk below them.

"When I realized I was pregnant and wouldn't need to use the clinic, I took the money I'd saved for their fees and did the same thing."

Mitch left the bed and moved behind her. "Great minds think alike," he started to say, but his mouth found the tantalizing spot on her neck that he loved to tease with his teeth.

"If we're thinking alike, what am I thinking now?"

"Something along the lines of you're almost afraid to be with me, because you know I'll want to explore the changes to your body. Or are you hesitant about sex, Avery? The books said..."

"Mitch, you were right the first time. I've changed dramatically. As to making love to you, that won't ever change. I've wanted you all along."

"Come back to bed," he told her in a soft tone with his lips to her ear, just before he pulled the straps of her slip from her shoulders. It fell to the floor at her feet and she turned toward him in the minimal light.

"My God, Avery, you're more beautiful now," he said, his hand guiding her toward the bed.

He paused to turn on a bedside light before lying down besidc her. His hand ran along her, from her neck to her ankle, stroking her naked flesh, remembering how she felt. Moving to straddle her legs, he let his hands fondle her larger breasts; his thumbs explored the changes in her nipples.

Only after a questioning glance did he lower his head towards her, his lips teasing more than tasting as he closed around her. Avery let out a sigh and moved her hands to his head, holding him to her breast.

"How sensitive are you?"

"I'm in heat, damn you, Mitchell. I've missed you. Please, come inside me, we can explore later, I need to feel you," she told him as her hand reached forward to cup his intense interest. As soon as he felt her hot skin against his, he moaned.

"Avery, you don't know the meaning of heat, yet." He dropped his mouth to hers and claimed her as he'd done at the lodge, taking what he wanted from her, what he needed to survive the onslaught of his feelings. He teased her with his mouth and his hands, working her into a fury that had her writhing under him.

His fingers explored her with caution at first. Finding her slick and ready, he let his mind forget for just a minute and he pushed inside her. Avery's inner muscles were so tight, flexing against just his finger made her cry out.

"Oh, God, I've missed you," he murmured as he dropped between her thighs, tasting the release he'd caused. It made him harder and he didn't stop to think before rising over her and slipping inside her heat.

"Mitch..." escaped from her lips as he entered her. His name on her lips spurred him to continue. Forcing himself to remember her condition, he pulled back to her entrance and watched her eyes fly open.

"Don't stop," she demanded, her voice husky with want, her need grasping him, pulling him deeper inside.

"Avery, it's been so long," he told her and realized she didn't care if it was quick, she wanted the release she now knew only he could provide her.

"Hurry, Mitch, we'll explore later, just...hurry now." Her fingers bit into his shoulders and he let his mind clear.

He felt each stroke as he moved against her moist heat and realized why she felt so different. An odd smile crossed his lips and she glanced up to see it, her eyes questioned him, her voice not able to form the words. His triumphant smile disappeared with his climax; he threw back his head and enjoyed his release.

As he relaxed above her, he shifted against her and she lost the last thread of control she'd managed to hold onto. Mitch watched her below him as she shifted and smiled, finally letting herself go. Her body froze under him for long seconds before she went slick around him. He managed to drop most of his weight onto his arms instead of crumbling on top of her.

"Damn it, Avery, you make me lose control so easily," he said, still pulling jagged breaths.

"And you never cease to amaze me." Her arms came up and dropped around him limply. "Now that we're beyond that, let's just relax and enjoy the rest of the night."

"Agreed," he told her, leaving the bed briefly, only to return with a bottle of water for them to share.

"Mitch, you can still drink, I'm not upset that I can't. It's all for a good cause."

"I know that, Avery, but it doesn't seem fair. I had wine with supper."

"But you usually enjoyed a glass after we..."

"Made love, yes, occasionally I do. But I'll skip the wine as long as you do, all right?"

"Your call. Now tell me, what was that strange smile about?"

"I realized it was the first time I'd been inside you unprotected."

Avery tossed back her head and laughed aloud. "If that were the case, we wouldn't be here right now."

"It's different in the pool or the hot tub and you know it." His lips, still cold from the water encircled her right nipple and she let out a small cry. "That's just to keep you in line."

"Oh, Mitch, keep me in line, again."

"My pleasure, Mrs. Avery Lambert Hamilton." His lips took hers under his and his hands slid along her back. Strong fingers held her to him and he knew he'd never feel this way with another woman, never find the extreme connection they made together.

Chapter Eleven

Ruth arrived just as room service delivered a fresh round of coffee and tea. Alexandra was due to arrive at work momentarily and they all knew as soon as she went to her office, she'd be told Mitch was in residence and wanted to speak to her. They also knew the odds were good that an employee would drop the bomb that his wife was with him, too.

Avery had dressed in a pant suit similar to the one she'd worn yesterday, only today it was a deep bronze color. She'd pulled the top and sides of her hair back but left the rest to fall down her back. She'd used minimal make-up and felt great. Sated from her night of loving Mitch and being loved by him, she realized today she felt that glow that people always associate with pregnant women. Ruth seemed to notice it, too; the wink that passed between them didn't go unnoticed by Mitch.

"Would you like to talk to her alone first, Mitch?" Avery asked.

"No, not unless this whole thing makes you uncomfortable."

"I just don't want the woman to walk in and see us lined up like a firing squad."

"After what she did to you, to us? You still want to guard her feelings?" Mitch ran his hand through the top of his hair and looked at her like she was crazy.

"Mitch, my being cruel toward her won't help anyone, especially me." She stood and walked to the balcony, letting herself get lost in the view. Hearing the knock, she steeled herself for what was to come. It wasn't how she'd pictured it and she waited by the balcony door to watch the scene unfold, forcing herself to push aside the memory of her last meeting with Alexandra.

Even then she felt the other woman was jealous and vindictive by nature, but rationalized she'd had the right, as Mitch's wife. In the last weeks, she decided that Alexandra was just a dark soul, lost to the good things in life, seeing only night instead of day unless it suited her purposes.

Alexandra all but slammed the door shut behind her as she entered Mitch's private suite. She was a vision of sleek elegance in a red Dior day suit and heavy perfume. Avery took a step back from the overpowering smell. Several gold bangle bracelets clanked with each movement she made.

"Mitch, what's going on? I'm hearing strange rumors. Tell me right now!"

Avery wondered if she'd stomp her size six foot on the carpet and laughed, looking down at her own size tens. Alexandra's perfume wafted through the air to Avery and she remembered being sick after Alex left her home, the smell overwhelming and sweet. Forcing back the renewed sick feeling, Avery breathed the fresh air deeply, trying to forget the image of the other woman in her living room.

"Alex, have a seat," Mitch said in a tone Avery had never heard before. He'd used a similar tone the night she wanted him to sign the affidavit but it lacked the authority she now heard. "We have some things to discuss."

"Ruth, what's going on? Is all this a horrible practical joke? Mitch, you know I've been waiting for you all these years, and now you come here with a mythical wife. Where ever did you get this crazy idea?" The younger woman settled back onto one of the sofas after pouring herself a cup of coffee, content to accept her version of the facts.

"Alexandra, I've realized lately I've been unfair to you. I've had you working harder than you should and that has seriously cut down on your social life."

"I don't need a social life, silly, I'm just biding my time until you realize I'm the right one for you."

"Alexandra, you're not. I've tried to tell you that for years and apparently in trying not to hurt your feelings, you've mistaken my intentions. I've never led you to believe that I'd one day marry you."

"That's part of your charm, dear, making me want you more every time you told me to find a better life." She drank from the cup and put it aside. "Mitch, you know…"

"No, Alex. I don't know. So why don't you tell me and my mother just what happened when I was in Australia and I sent you to Las Vegas to help with the opening."

"I don't know what you mean. The opening was a huge success and even you said so."

"What else happened when I was away? And, Alex, think carefully about what you say next. I'm looking for the truth. I'll accept nothing less."

"I don't know what you're referring to."

"Did I receive any personal mail?"

Mitch sat back in the club chair, his right ankle crossed over his left knee, the dark blue of his pants in direct contrast to the white shirt he wore. His dark eyes were darker than usual and even from her position on the balcony Avery could see that Ruth was disappointed by the younger woman's attitude. Watching her decide how to get out of the situation, Avery hadn't expected anger.

"I only did what I thought was best. You don't need some gold-digging floozy to extort money from you. How cruel a woman did you pick up, Mitch, thinking she could blackmail you with hints about a baby. I knew right away she had to be one of your quick affairs, so I dealt with her, just like I deal with all the small problems that come up."

"Or the so-called small problems that get in your way?"

"*Really,* you'd think she was important. An Amazon of a woman, good God, Mitch, she reminded me of an obese basketball player. You must have been desperately lonely when she seduced you." Alex sighed and rolled her eyes at him. "When we finally marry, I assume you'll curtail your extra curricular activities, dear?"

She flashed him a smile and Avery decided it was probably the one she'd used all her life to wrap men around her well-manicured finger.

"We won't ever marry, Alex. I've tried to tell you that for years and you've ignored me. Now I understand it's time for you to go out in the world and find yourself a mate."

"What are you saying? I want you. Ruth, tell him I'm the right one for him."

"No, Alexandra. I don't feel you are. I think you've had a crush on Mitch since you were a child. But you should have grown out of it and started your own life."

"Ruth, I thought you of all people would be on my side."

"Then you were wrong, I'm not taking sides. I only want what's best for everyone involved. It's time you found out what you're really meant to do with your life. And it's time for Mitch to get on with his, without you in the foreground or the background."

"*Ruth*!"

"I spoke with your mother last night, told her our good news about Mitch eloping. She seemed relieved. Even she spoke about you moving on."

There was a long, protracted silence among them while Alexandra tried to figure out just what had happened. It didn't take long for her to put the pieces together once Avery came into the room and walked directly to Mitch, sitting on the arm of his chair, her hand on his shoulder.

"I know you've already met, but I'll introduce you anyway. Alexandra, this is my wife, Avery Lambert Hamilton." Avery forced her face to remain still, to wipe the smug smile that wanted to appear from her lips. She stared the woman down, her eyes not leaving her face.

"We've met," Avery said, and watched as Alex tried a new approach.

"All right, so obviously I made a mistake. It didn't keep you two apart, so no harm done, right?" Her attempt to lighten their moods didn't work and her smile faded.

"You've made a drastic mistake, assuming to know my private life better than I do. I won't take a chance on trusting you ever again with my wife or my children."

"Children? Surely she can't be pregnant by you, you can't..."

"Life has a strange way of working things out, Alexandra. Avery is my wife and carrying my child. End of story. If you run into her ever again, I expect you to treat her with the utmost respect and the same goes for my children."

"Mitch, if you really want her, then fine, but that doesn't mean I can't continue to run the hotel for you." The hopeful look on her face faded quickly and she narrowed her gaze on Avery. "This is your doing. You're afraid if I'm around he'll want me instead of a fat cow of a woman like you. And he will, one day."

"That's enough!" Mitch growled at her. "That's exactly why you won't be around to hassle Avery or myself. We won't accept displays like that again, do you understand me?"

She'd turned her back on him, her hands

clutching her upper arms. “Alexandra, I’ve made a few calls. There’s an envelope on the side table. Take it. It’s a year’s severance pay and the names of a few acquaintances that could use your talents in their hotels.”

She swung around in disbelief. “You really mean to send me away?”

“As far as possible. You’re lucky I didn’t drag your name through the mud. Instead, I’m offering you a chance at a future. I don’t care if you travel or find a new job. I only care that you don’t do it in my home towns, which means no Atlantic City, Las Vegas, Lake Tahoe, or the Napa Valley area.”

Avery glanced to Mitch when he said Napa Valley but didn’t interrupt. There would be plenty of time later to find out what he meant.

“You can’t be serious?” Alex’s voice took on the tone of a spoiled child.

“Stay away from the coast of Australia where the new project is, too. And Manhattan is Avery’s territory.” Mitch stood to his full height and took Avery’s hand. She rose next to him, her free hand on her belly, joining with Mitch’s. “The one thing in this life I really wanted was Avery and our family. You tried to destroy that for all of us. I don’t ever want to see you again.” He hesitated before adding, “Be careful what you do tell people, Alex, I have eyes and ears in places you’d never imagine.”

She glanced at him with narrowed eyes and a bloodthirsty grin. He stared and didn’t turn away. Somehow she knew it was best not to attack him on that front.

“It would be best to accept the reality of the situation, Alex,” Ruth started. “Nobody would think twice if you decided a change of scenery was in order after Mitch’s elopement.”

“You can’t mean this; I had our future all worked out.”

“Not with me,” he answered in a softer tone.

"The company car will be transferred to your name next week. Consider it a bonus. But don't think to cross me, ever again. And don't ever think about harming Avery or my family. I'll come after you myself if you do." Mitch gave Alex one final look of distain and shook his head in disgust.

"I'll pack up my things from the office."

"Your things have been packed and loaded into your car. I've also taken possession of the custody agreement you didn't return to Avery when you brought back her letters. It only makes me wonder what else you've taken from my desk." He didn't add that he'd also taken a stash of sensitive business material she'd squirreled away in her office safe.

"How did you find..." she started, only to be cut off by his exasperated tone.

"Hank's waiting for you and I'll expect you to give him your keys and go quietly. Your call, Alex. You can make a scene or go quietly with some dignity. All the codes have been changed and the staff alerted to your moving on. Don't try anything stupid or vindictive, I won't stand for it."

In a last fit of fury, she grabbed a crystal vase from the sideboard and turned with it in her hand. She eyed first Ruth, then Avery, standing at Mitch's side.

"Think carefully, Alexandra. That vase and dignity don't go together."

"I hate you, I hate all of you!" she cried as she pitched the vase towards the center of the seating area.

Mitch pulled Avery behind him to shield her and Ruth had backed up the moment she grabbed the glass. The door to the suite opened and Hank Waters stood there, a second man behind him in a dark suit and dark glasses. Mitch only had to nod his head slightly and Hank had Alex by the arm, tugging her out of the room, trying to calm her with soothing words. The other man nodded to them and took the envelope from the bureau before closing the door behind him.

"You all right?" Mitch asked, pulling back to check on Avery. She nodded with a strange look on her face. "Mom, you okay?"

"Yes. I remembered her from when she was a child. She never outgrew her temper tantrums."

Avery froze and finally dropped into the chair behind her, letting out a sigh. It turned into a smile and with one glance to Ruth then Mitch, she finally started to laugh out loud. It was cleansing for them all and it wasn't until there was another knock on the door that she reined back her emotions. Housekeeping entered quietly and cleaned up the broken glass while Ruth led Avery to the balcony.

"I'm going to change and go for a run along the boardwalk; her perfume is very heavy," Avery said. She left Mitch and Ruth on the balcony and changed into sweats quickly. Pausing in the doorway while she worked her hair into a braid, Avery told them both she'd be back in an hour.

Mitch moved to follow her but Ruth held his arm.

"Let her go, Mitch. She doesn't like to think she's the reason for Alex getting fired."

"Alex deciding my future is the reason I let her go."

"I know and so does Avery. Only it all traces back to her, so ultimately she feels some responsibility. And you have to learn to take a step back and let her breathe on her own, before she boots you out the door for smothering her. I wasn't kidding yesterday when I told you to take your leash from around her neck. Just because she wears your ring doesn't make her incompetent in any way and the longer you treat her as a child, the less time she'll spend with you."

"How did you get so all knowing and wise?" he teased his mother.

"I'm a woman, and I was married to your father. Enough said." Ruth strolled through the living room and grabbed her purse from the table. "Tell Avery to call me when she gets back if she's still up to some shopping. I have some phoning to do."

****

Mitch sat on the balcony staring at the ocean below him. His mother had been right; he'd been just short of possessive and he knew it would drive Avery away. One of the things that drew him to her was her independent nature and her brash attitude toward being helpless or naive. It made her the woman he fell in love with. And to keep her, he'd have to check his well-meant, smothering intentions at the door.

When she returned later, his mind relaxed slightly, but he didn't tell her; instead he passed along his mother's invitation. Avery made a quick call and headed back to the bedroom. He didn't dare enter the bath while she was in there, knowing one look at her and they'd never leave the room. He finished some business calls and was ready to head downstairs when she came out half an hour later.

"I'll be in the main office for a while; my cell will be on if you need me."

"That's all? No third degree or time limits?" she teased.

"I'm working on not being possessive, Avery. Cut me some slack. I finally have you back in my life and I just want to protect you, both of you. So until I get my act together, don't hate me for wanting to take care of you."

"I don't hate you for it; it's just such a foreign concept for me. I'm used to being on my own, Mitch. I've been on my own since my parent's car crash six years ago. I depend on myself to survive. Beyond the baby, any relationship with you will be intense and we both have to learn to adapt to each other."

"You did a lot of thinking while you ran," he

said.

"And apparently you did, too. I'm not running away from you, Mitch. I promise you, I won't do that, but please don't smother me with good intentions." She pulled back and stared at him just before she let her fingers run along his jaw where she'd landed him a surprise hit after finding out he owned the hotel in Las Vegas. "I might get testy again and you wouldn't want to have to explain to your staff how you got a black eye from your bride!"

"No, the jaw was hard enough to explain away," he told her, just before he kissed her. "Have a good afternoon," he said and left her side.

"Mitch?"

"Yes?" She moved toward him then hesitated. He waited while she made up her mind what she was going to say and wasn't sure he wanted to know.

"I'll see you later," she finally blurted out.

"I love you, Avery." His words circled around them as he left the room.

Chapter Twelve

Walking the boardwalk later that night, it wasn't uncomfortable for Mitch to have his arm around Avery. They had a late supper with Ruth before she diplomatically said her good byes and assured Avery she'd be a presence in all their lives. Avery finally let go of the guilt she carried over Alex and her ultimate dismissal.

"In the mood to talk or would you rather just be quiet?"

"It depends on the subject," she said, her voice light.

"You mentioned you have meetings on Wednesday. What kind of schedule will you have for the next few months?"

Avery went on to tell him about the few jobs she was finishing. If all went according to plan, she'd be finished with everything just around the end of her eighth month. She'd made a conscious decision not to book any jobs until after the baby was at least three months old.

"Where would you like to have the baby?" His question didn't surprise her, but to her there wasn't any other option.

"In Manhattan of course; it's where all my doctors are."

"What about after, for the first few months, where would you like to spend that time? We have your townhouse, the suite here or in Las Vegas, or the lodge?"

"I hadn't really thought about it, Mitch. Up until two weeks ago my choices were made. Done deal. Now I guess I'll have to rethink some of them. What about you, what's your schedule like?"

He told her about the project on the Australian coast and the small residential hotel he was looking at in San Francisco. He pulled her to the side and brushed a strand of hair from her cheek.

"Want to work on that for a few months after Jr. is born?"

"I don't know. I have no idea."

"Don't panic, Avery, it was just a thought."

"What other thoughts have you been having?" Her voice left no room for him to think about business and he gave her his sly smile. "I'm thinking I'd like to go for a swim before we turn in for the night. Interested in joining me?"

"Always, but we'll have to check with the owner about his policy on bathing suits."

"Or maybe we could talk him into closing the area for a few hours."

"I like the way your mind works."

****

Avery's strong arms and legs propelled her through the warmed water as Mitch kept up beside her, lap for lap. Only when she paused in the deep end did he stop beside her, his arms going around her. He'd spent the last twenty minutes watching her and it was too much to ask of him not to touch her. She accepted his kisses and his wandering hands for several minutes before pulling away.

She wore a black, two-piece, stretchy tank top style bathing suit with matching full black bottoms that covered her completely, yet rode just under her belly. The top moved easily over her growing body, revealing a few inches of baby to his warm hand. It was easy to slip it under the material and let his palm feel her in such an intimate way. It wasn't sexual but it was. It wasn't as if he was touching her indecently, yet his hand on her and her baby made her feel safe and protected. Only when his fingers traced higher towards her full breast did she pull back to watch his eyes.

"Mitch, the security cameras," she said, just as his hand found her nipple.

"Turned off," he whispered, his mouth close to hers, taking her on a roller coaster ride of a kiss so intimate it left her warm and just short of weak.

"Are you sure?" she whispered. "I'd not like to think we're on candid camera." The restraint in her voice weakened as her fingers dug into his shoulders. Avery let her body float back on the water and was just reaching to Mitch when she jolted and let her body go under the water, floating to the top again to find his worried face.

"Avery, are you all right?"

She swam to the side of the pool and used the ladder to pull herself from the water. Mitch hoisted his body onto the side of the pool and was there to question her.

"Avery?"

"Take me upstairs, Mitch, right now." She tossed a towel toward him and grabbed one for herself, blotting the moisture from the long strands of her hair. He quickly dropped a toweling robe over her shoulders and grabbed his own.

"I'm all right, Mitch, I just want to be in a private place."

They took the private corridor back to the elevator; he didn't question her until they were back in the room.

"What happened in the pool, Avery, is everything all right?" She gave him an odd look and slipped past him to the shower, rinsing the chlorine from her hair and skin and he slipped in behind her just as she was getting out. Setting a record time for showering, he found her waiting on the bed for him, propped against a pile of pillows, her wet hair spread out behind her on a towel she'd laid over the pillows.

"Avery?" Mitch walked toward her naked form, pausing beside the bed. "You are the most beautiful sight I've ever seen, like a Botticelli master."

"Mitch, in the top drawer, there's a small brown paper bag; would you get it for me?"

He found the item quickly and had no idea what the flat box inside it contained. He handed it to her and sat gently beside her, watching her pull the box from the bag. Lying naked stretched across his bed, the sight of her made him harden under the towel he'd tucked around his waist, tenting it for her view.

Avery held her hand on her lower belly. She watched Mitch's face but didn't speak. When she did, her voice was strained by emotion as she tried to hold back the onslaught of tears that threatened to spill out. He was confused but gave her time to compose herself.

"Mitch, I'm all right. Don't panic," she whispered.

He relaxed somewhat beside her but didn't move away; rather he studied her intently as her hand moved over their baby. When she'd managed to control her emotions she pulled the stethoscope from the box and put it to her ears, the cold end making her nipples harden on contact with her skin. As soon as he saw the device he relaxed beside her. He watched her place the tip in several places and then a wide smile cross her lips. She handed him the top of the scope and relaxed back onto the pillows. Understanding, he took her offering and placed it to his ears, his hand covering hers where she held the end.

Michael Mitchell Hamilton was blown away. The sound was more of a whooshing noise than a heartbeat, but it was strong and rhythmic, fast. He closed his eyes and listened to his child's heart beat within Avery and he didn't try to hold back his tears or emotions. They stayed that way for a long time, Avery spread back on the pillows with Mitch listening to her belly. Her hands moved over her skin and again she jolted. He opened his eyes and found he was looking at her tearstained cheeks.

She took his hand and pulled it to her left side, pressing it against her with her own hand. "I don't know if you can feel that?" she whispered.

He moved his fingers around and shook his head.

"It's not a real kick, it's more of a fluttering feeling, like butterfly wings against me."

"I can't feel it," he said, disappointment apparent in his voice.

"It's early for you to feel her, I've only felt this a few times before and I wasn't sure I was really feeling her. Tonight, I realized it was her moving inside me."

Mitch threw the scope aside on the bed and drew her to his chest. They held each other in the embrace for a long time, neither wanting to let go. Finally, Avery pulled back and reached to the table for a tissue.

"I didn't mean to go to pieces like that, it's just..."

"God, Avery, do you have any idea how wonderful this is, even if I can't feel him move yet, just to hear his heart beat is incredible. Is that why we stopped at the drug store?"

"Yes, a friend told me she'd been able to hear her baby's heart beat after the fourth month. I figured it was worth a try since you missed the last doctor's appointment."

"I don't want to miss any more."

She nodded and wiped his cheek. "Thank you," she whispered as she drew his mouth to hers. "Mitch, are you sure about all this?"

"Oh, Avery, more than sure. It's what my heart

desired all my life and I never allowed myself to imagine it could happen for me. How did I get so lucky? First you and now our baby."

"I hope that never changes, Mitch. Promise me, if you decide you've had enough of us, you'll tell me before it ruins us."

"I'm not going to change, Avery. I'm almost forty and you've given me a second chance at the life I always coveted."

"Mitch, I do love you, and I love our child, and I'm…"

"Emotionally drained from the last few weeks of me acting like an ass," he teased.

"Yes and no. It's more that I'm afraid to believe in us, it's all too perfect. I keep waiting for something to happen to taint us," she admitted.

"That's why I felt it was important for you to be here when I confronted Alexandra. I didn't want any unresolved ideas or feelings between us. I wanted you to understand I never gave her any encouragement on a personal level."

They relaxed against the headboard for a while, his arms around her. There was no thought to her nakedness sprawled beside him, or his beside her. It was the most natural thing for them to lie together, both feeling the life they'd created.

"Mitch, can you do something for me?" she asked her voice low.

"Anything," he whispered back.

"Call room service. I'm starving!"

He laughed at her before pulling from her side, shaking his head as he reached for the telephone beside the bed. "And here I was hoping it was something sexual."

"It could be, but not until you feed us both!"

Avery slipped from the bed and found her chemise, drawing it over her head and letting the silk slip over her. Her hair had air dried and he watched as she slowly combed the tangles from it while they waited for their food. The late night news had gone off the air by the time they were full.

She took his hand and drew him back toward the bedroom. "I'm content with food, now make me content in other ways," she told him, as she slipped the straps from her shoulders and let the silk float to the floor.

He followed behind her, pausing only to take the rose from the room service tray with him. Using the soft petals, he drove her into a frenzied lust running them over her skin, his lips tracing the path. The whole time he loved her he had to hold back from jumping in and taking what he wanted. Somehow Avery seemed to understand and accepted his gift. Only when he'd driven her over the edge of sanity with his hands and lips did he pull her toward him, letting himself sink inside the heated tunnel he'd come to know as home. Their loving was slow and intense, each stroke or touch a kiss in itself.

Mitch had experienced his share of women in his life, but something about Avery made him connect on a different level. She created an inner warmth and feeling of well-being inside him that he'd never known before. The idea made him throb inside her and she hurried his movements to complete the want he'd built within her. When she found her second release, he let himself go, following her into the safe place she always drew him to. Mitch rolled to the side and she moved beside him, his arm going protectively around her.

"Avery, I love you," he whispered, his lips to her ear. "And you are my wife."

She stiffened to move away but he held her in place, not stifling the laugh he knew would annoy her.

"We'll see," she topped him with and his fingers dipped lower towards her junction, skimming just above her want. "Keep that up and we won't sleep at all."

"My exact intention," he told her before slipping down her body to claim her again in the dark of the night.

****

Avery spent a relaxing day exploring the boardwalk of Atlantic City, by herself. She'd enjoyed the time she spent with Ruth Hamilton and she knew she was in love with Mitch, but it seemed the last few weeks she hadn't had a moment to herself. She knew once the baby was born, she never would again. Mitch seemed reluctant to leave her on her own today but didn't want the confrontation. She smiled as she wandered past the shop windows, remembering their words. Heated words she decided, not a fight.

"I'll rearrange my schedule to come with you." His voice told her it was a done deal. That had set her on edge as soon as they left the shower that morning. They dressed around each other but the mood was thick. Finally she just told him straight out, before she let the resentment build inside her.

"Mitch, I want the day to myself." There, she'd said it aloud. Lightning bolts hadn't appeared through the ceiling and struck her down. However, from the look on his face, they might as well have. "Don't pout," she told him, forcing her voice to soften. "It's doesn't mean I don't want you at all. I just need a few hours for myself."

"Am I being relegated to bedtime, Avery? Are you telling me I have no place in your daily life, company at night only?"

She'd swung around to face him, the confusion apparent. He studied her in the mirror over the sink as he ran the razor along his chin. Avery studied him, his hostility suddenly making her stand taller on her frame before answering.

"No, it simply means that for a woman who's lived alone for the last ten years of her life, you're a very overpowering influence to be around." She'd left the bath before he could answer.

"What the hell does that mean?" He stormed past her to the bureau and started to pull on underwear while they talked. It didn't escape his vision that she pulled on a pink bra and panties under the jeans and comfortable sweater.

"It simply means that in a very short period of time we've started living together, and I'm not sure I like it just yet. It's all so fast Mitch. Two weeks ago I thought you hated me and never wanted anything to do with me again. You turn up in the grocery with demands and confuse me more. Now this whole fiasco with Alexandra getting fired and loving you all this time. And since we left Manhattan last Friday morning, I've had all of three hours to myself."

She continued to apply a light coat of make-up, mostly mascara and lip color. Brushing her hair, she glanced to him, watching him button a fresh white shirt. "Mitch, I'm alone most of the time. It's not that I don't want you around, it's just that twenty four-seven is overwhelming."

"Well we wouldn't want to overwhelm the mother-to-be."

Avery slowly closed the cap on her lipstick and turned toward him. "Just exactly what does that mean?" Her arms folded across her and came to rest on her belly.

"It means, Avery, that you're not the only one whose life has been turned upside down in the last two weeks. So has mine. But I still want you with me, all the time. I'm sorry if I'm stifling you, but I feel like I missed so much already and I don't want to miss any more."

"Missed the baby, not necessarily me?"

"No, you're a package deal." As soon as Mitch said the words aloud he acknowledged it was a mistake with a nod of his head. He watched several things pass over her face and she said none of them.

She turned back to the mirror and started to braid her hair.

"I'm sorry, that didn't come out right."

"Maybe it came out completely right, Mitch."

"Avery, we're both trying to be so careful not to hurt the other one that we're tiptoeing around each other at times. Not all the time, when we're alone and the sun goes down we know how to relate to each other."

"Sex," she whispered to herself.

"That, too, but after dark, the business goes away. Right now, I'm wondering how to get everything done so you don't have to wait around for me."

"Mitch, don't you see, that's my point. Tomorrow we'll go back to New York. Wednesday I have appointments all day. I don't plan to cancel any of them and I don't expect you to be tagging along, any more than I'd expcct you to take me to the office with you today."

He stopped to watch her finish her hair. "Which leaves us exactly where?"

"It should leave us both with being able to have our careers and our personal lives at the same time. We both have to readjust our thinking." She moved to the loveseat near the fireplace and reached out a hand to him. When he reluctantly joined her, she drew a breath before speaking.

"Mitch, if we were any normal couple, we'd have dated and then spent some time engaged. We would have worked past all this by now. Other than two brief meetings at Jack's and our dinner in Las Vegas, besides the week at the lodge, we've not been together.

"Granted, our time at the lodge was intense, but you have to remember that for the last three and a half months I've been under the impression that you didn't want anything to do with me." He started to interrupt but she brought her finger to his lips to quiet him. "I'm not saying it's your fault, but it's a fact. In the last two weeks you've come into my life like a tornado and I haven't touched down since. I just want a few hours a day to myself to remember who I am. I don't think I'm asking a lot. I acknowledge the amount of freedom your career will bring to our family and I'm looking forward to it, but overnight you've become...an appendage. I don't know how better to explain it. I don't mean to hurt your feelings or complain, I'm just trying to make you understand that the more you push at me the further I'll recede. I know me, Mitch. You have to give me space."

Avery watched him drop back on the cushion, his fingers rubbing his temples. When his cell phone rang, he ignored it. When it rang a second time he picked it up and shut it off.

"So I'm overbearing and overpowering. What else? When we were at the lodge you didn't seem to mind my being around you all the time."

"Ahh, but you weren't, were you? Every afternoon or that one morning, you went to your study and worked for a few hours. Those few hours a day is all I'm looking for now. When work starts, I'll be able to tailor my schedule, which will help. We can both work in the mornings or the afternoons, whatever we want, but I need to be a viable human being beyond being a vessel for your daughter."

"Son."

"We'll see."

"We could find out, put an end to the debate." Mitch dropped his hand from his forehead finally and relaxed back on the couch.

"Too easy, Mr. Hamilton. I don't want to take the fight out of you, I just want to be able to go to neutral corners for a few hours a day."

"I'll try to accommodate your wishes, Mrs. Hamilton!"

"And about that, are you going to let me off the

hook finally or what?"

"Or what," he told her before dropping a kiss on her cheek and rising from beside her. "Avery, the timing sucks, but if I wait until tonight like I'd planned, you might think I did this for other reasons." He went to his bureau and pulled out a black box. Standing behind the sofa she sat on, he handed it to her. "I was going to give it to you at supper, but I'd rather you understand it came with love, not guilt over our fight."

"That wasn't a fight, Mitch. That was clearing the air in a slightly higher voice than usual." She tried to hold back a smile but didn't.

"That's what that was. Well then I'm disappointed. Here I was, looking forward to make-up sex tonight." He bent to drop a light kiss on her lips. "Open your present."

Avery was leery of the gift. The ring she wore now still felt as strange as it had from the beginning. She'd left it on because it came from Mitch with a promise of fidelity and love.

"Mitch, I don't need presents."

"I know, but I wanted you to have this."

Slowly she opened the box to find a diamond tennis style bracelet lying on the silk. She pulled it from the box and held it to her ring and understood. The center stone was three carats and the two flanking it were solid one carat stones. The bracelet was a circle of matching one carat stones. It was a stunning piece and the idea that he'd had it made with her ring brought tears to her eyes.

"I don't need presents, Mitch. I just need to know we're doing the right thing for our child," she told him as she turned to kneel on the sofa, reaching over the back of it to pull him to her. His large hands steadied her and held her tight.

"We'll adjust, Avery. And after the baby's born, we'll adjust again. We just have to keep our sense of humor." He pulled back and wiped the tears from her cheeks with the pads of his thumbs before taking the platinum from her fingers and clasping it around her wrist.

"It's beautiful, Mitch."

"Wear it, Avery. I don't want it stuck in the box in the back of the safe only to be brought out on special occasions."

"But Mitch…"

"God forbid anyone ever tried to take it from you, I assume you'll have the common sense to hand it over quickly and not fight over some cold stones that decorate your wrist. Understand?"

She glanced from him to the bracelet and back to him. "Avery, these stones, they can be replaced. You can't." He kissed her again and this time they both wanted to prove to the other that they understood, and would try to work through their new lives together.

****

Avery spent the morning viewing three other suites that were available for Mitch to take over. Currently, he used a two-bedroom suite with a wet bar and dining and living areas. The three that she saw today all had larger kitchens and four bedrooms. The last one impressed her the most; the living area was larger and there was a den towards the front of the suite that could be turned into a play area. It had the same view as his old suite and was only one floor farther up. She'd made some quick notes about changing out a few things but knew the suite could work for them.

After that, she went walking and on her way back spied a small brown teddy bear in the window of a store that she couldn't resist. He was soft and cuddly, with no parts to pull or bite off. His facial expressions had been embroidered on instead of using buttons. She bought it without a second thought and continued on her way.

Carrying a soft, doughy pretzel, she turned into

a store and ran smack into Alexandra. They both held their stance for a minute, then Avery moved to the side. She felt the other woman grab at her shoulder and turned around, peering down at her, hoping to intimidate her out of a confrontation.

"It's all your fault," Alex said, her voice angry.

"That you have a dark soul, no, it's not. That you decided to take another person's life into your hands? No, that's not my fault either."

"He was mine until you came along."

"He was never yours, or he wouldn't be mine now." Avery knew her words were curt and they hurt, but she didn't relent. She let this woman come between her and Mitch once before, she refused to stand back and let it happen again. Something passed over Alexandra's face, a look of realization and hate mixed together. Drawing a breath she added, "If you really have feelings for Mitch, then you'd want him to be happy."

Turning from any further confrontation, Avery moved away with the tourists and let herself get lost in the crowd. Somehow she felt better but slightly sickened. She dropped onto a bench near the hotel's main entrance and stayed there a long time, the teddy bear in her hands.

That was how Mitch found her, sitting watching the ocean with a brown teddy bear clutched in her hands. He slipped beside her on the bench and spoke quickly.

"I didn't come looking for you," he said in a defensive tone, relaxing when she laughed outright at him. "Avery?"

"I ran into Alexandra and couldn't help but wonder what our lives would have been like if she'd gotten her way."

Mitch settled beside her, his arm going around her shoulders and pulling her to him. "What did she say?"

"Not much. I told her if she truly cared for you,

she'd want you to be happy, even if that meant it was with me. I didn't give her a chance to answer."

"I don't want to even go there and you shouldn't either. We make our choices from now on, and we're the only ones who count, along with Jr. there." He pulled the bear from her hands and gave him a quick inspection before handing him back. "What did you think of the suites you saw? Will any of them work or do you want to design something?"

She went on to talk through her ideas for the third suite and he took her back to it, walking through the apartment as she described the minor changes. It felt odd to walk through the hotel and know the employees were checking them out, mainly checking her out. Mitch introduced her to several people they met along the way. Everyone seemed friendly and congratulated them both.

Only one woman, Rebecca, seemed to be straining to smile at their introduction. Later Mitch told her she was Alexandra's best friend. He also explained that she'd been given a choice to stay on in her current position as long as her attitude didn't infect the hotel, or she was free to cancel her contract and move on. Hank would keep an eye on the situation and handle it if he felt she was becoming a problem.

"I agree on the suite. I'll have it handled this week. Next time we come back here, we'll be at home." He pulled her into his arms and hesitated before asking, "What about when we're in Manhattan? Should I get a hotel suite there, too?"

She knew he was joking but his hesitation made her realize how on edge he was. "Only for the nights you piss me off," she answered and kissed him quickly before pulling from his arms. "Oh no. It's not our room yet!" she told him with a laugh when he got that gleam in his eye. "If you take me back to our room, you might just get lucky!"

Almost dragging her, he hurried them into his

suite and let her take him quickly with an intensity he remembered from the lodge. It was a joining of souls and bodies that was intense and satisfying. Lying spent on the living room sofa, Avery straddled his lap with her head resting on his shoulder; she finally felt all things were right in the world. She just didn't know how long they'd last.

Later that night, she allowed him to open the parcel he'd carried from her home. It was a watercolor landscape that she'd finished just a few weeks before the holidays. It was meant to be his Christmas gift but, after not hearing back from him, she hadn't shipped it. Now it would finally come to its rightful owner. She'd been proud of the piece; it was a major departure from her normal work, but a satisfying one. Avery poured all her love and pent up emotions she carried home from the lodge at Lake Tahoe into the piece. Mitch was beyond pleased with it; his facial expression was all she needed to know she'd been right about his gift.

****

Leaving him the next day was beyond what either of them could have imagined. Mitch drove her back into the city and helped her into the apartment. They brought Chinese food and ate from the cartons hours later after a lazy bath and an even lazier evening of making love. They compared their schedules and she knew the three weeks he'd be away would be difficult for her now. In the past, only her time mattered, now with the weeks stretching in front of them, they both seemed depressed.

"It's easy," he teased. "Just give up your life and follow mine." He followed it with a quick kiss and defused her quick anger.

"Or you could give up yours…" When he rolled away from her she sat up, somehow knowing she'd hit a sore spot. "Mitch, what did I say?"

"Avery, I want you to come to California with me. I mentioned Napa valley; I'd like to show you something there. I figured we could tour it when you viewed the San Francisco job."

"Mitch, what's going on?"

"See the place first, all right? If you don't like it, we'll find something else."

"Find what else? You're talking in circles Mitch," she told him.

"I found a place, an old estate. It needs a lot of work, Avery. The house needs to be completely rebuilt and the fields and the vines were left for years. It's been tied up in an estate situation and it was left to go to seed."

"Are you telling me you want to turn it into a home or hotel or that you want to become a wine maker?"

"Both."

Avery left the bed and pulled on her dark blue robe. "I'm gonna need coffee for this. Meet me downstairs and we'll talk." She left him naked and alone in her bedroom and it felt right. He joined her a few minutes later, carrying the tray to the window seat that looked out on the street below. It was almost deserted, only the low hum of city noise intruded on his telling her about the old place. She managed to ask intelligent questions, she thought, considering it was the first time she'd heard about it and how little she knew about wine. She focused on the idea that he wanted a place to call his own. Not just to build or manage. He wanted something tangible to go to every day.

"That would mean starting over for me, too," she whispered, realizing how much work it took to build her name and reputation over the years. The contacts and friends, the professional people she knew she could depend on, and who not to work with again. All of it seemed slightly overwhelming. Hadn't she worked so hard to get to this point in her life so she could coast a bit when the baby was little? It was too much to comprehend at the moment.

Chapter Thirteen

For weeks life went by in a haze for Avery. Mitch flew in and out on a steady basis. She'd been stunned by how much she missed him when he left for three weeks after their trip to Atlantic City. They spoke often on the telephone but there was an odd feeling deep inside her when they didn't connect.

Those nights she tossed and turned in her lonely bed. He told her he was trying to finish the Australian project so he wouldn't have to leave her after the baby was born. He also promised to take her there for their honeymoon after Jr. arrived. She wanted to go sooner but the timing was wrong for her to make such long flights at this point in her pregnancy.

They managed to get almost two weeks in California, spending a few days in San Francisco, where Mitch ultimately decided to let the hotel go. Beyond what it needed cosmetically, the building needed major reconstruction and he didn't see the return. They had, however, spent the rest of their time in the Napa Valley area.

For Avery, it was a dream come true. She never thought she could love another place as much as she loved Manhattan. But something about the abandoned estate drew her, called to her. They wandered the fields of vines that had been left to seed and made love beside them under the blue sky. She spent many hours just staring at the old ramshackle home, its stone walls sturdy, waiting for a second chance to house life and laughter.

Mitch took to leaving her alone during those times, sensing she was bonding with the house. He spent his time bonding with the vines and the earth. He read everything he could get his hands on and was relieved when they finally closed the deal. Bringing her back to what was now their run-down winery and estate later that night, they ate the picnic he brought and lay under the stars on blankets.

Their times together were magical. Mitch truly seemed to love her, no matter what her size or disposition. Lately, she'd gotten testy a few times with him. They learned to banter their way out of a fight and learned to fight it out when it was important to them both. It would take years to bring the place back to its original beauty but it was something they both wanted. They talked about their children running through the fields and probably hating the business when they grew up. And they made a conscious decision not to press for the label to be handed down if it wasn't wanted.

They laughed together about the label. Both knew it would be years before they bottled their first vintage and longer before the place ever turned a profit. Neither of them cared. They were building a home, not just a label. And neither of them ventured into naming the winery yet, considering how much trouble they were having discussing names for the baby. By mutual consent, they let the winery name alone.

With Mitch still holding interests in both Atlantic City and Las Vegas, they knew he'd have to travel some but hoped it wouldn't be too much time spent away from her and the baby. They'd manage, he promised and she believed him. The only nagging that still kept coming back to her was leaving everything she'd built in Manhattan.

Mitch hadn't pressed her to sell her townhouse; instead he wanted her to keep it for a while, maybe ultimately rent it out for a few years. That made her feel better, but still she had reservations. They fought and bantered over their "proxy" situation and both left it alone. She thought often to call her lawyer and ask him to check it out, but never got around to actually making the call. It was a quiet reminder of their promises.

****

Ruth spent a few days with Avery in the city, shopping for baby items and generally being company for her while Mitch was away on what they both hoped would be the last leg of his Australian deal. The resort was coming along almost on schedule and after the baby was born, they'd vacation there. She'd seen the photos and drawings and loved the laid-back atmosphere he was trying to accomplish. The nursery had taken shape over the last months: her mural complete, the crib put together, all waiting for Jr.

Mitch managed to sit in on a few of the birthing classes she attended and it amazed her how well informed he really was on the topic. And she let herself laugh to fulfillment when he almost passed out during the video they watched in class. That dose of reality had them both speechless for a few days.

Avery managed to finish her jobs on a reasonable schedule, knowing the two contractors she'd been working with didn't want to upset her in her condition. And what a condition it was. Avery never would have believed her body could change the way it did. Every part of her stretched to accommodate the soccer player she and Mitch had made together.

He'd been wonderful during the remainder of her pregnancy, feeding her anything she wanted and going along with her whims and emotional spurts.

He even adjusted to letting her have some time to herself each day. Those few hours they spent apart made seeing him again so much more precious. Her feet were swollen, much like the rest of her and she was glad Ruth had gone back to New Jersey. It wasn't that she didn't want her around; it was just that she wanted some time alone for herself. For four days she enjoyed it, then all hell broke loose.

****

The envelope had an Australian postmark but no return address. Inside of it were several photographs. Photographs of Mitch with his arm around a slim blonde woman. They were candids taken from a distance, both Mitch and his friend wet from the swimming pool they stood before. Avery was crushed. She turned them over several times, not finding any notation on the backs. All she saw was Mitch, obviously enjoying himself with another woman. The idea nagged at her but she tried to think calmly and rationally. Maybe they were old friends was one idea. What bothered her more was the way he seemed to be looking at the woman, the way he used to look at her.

The fact that there was no note, no words or writing at all was puzzling. Just the damning photos, three of them in all. She tried to call Mitch that afternoon with no luck. When he finally got back to her that night, he was short with her.

"What is it, Avery? Is the baby okay?"

Not *are you okay and the baby* or the other way around, just *is the baby okay.* She was annoyed before his call; now she was just pissed. Trying to keep their conversation on an even keel, it didn't help when he told her he'd be stuck there for at least another week. He offered to have Ruth stay with her but she refused. There was nothing to say. Beyond strained, Avery had cut him short.

"It's obvious I've become a nuisance, Mitch. I won't call again. I wouldn't want to intrude on your private time."

"What the hell does that mean?"

"Ask your girlfriend!" she hollered into the receiver, unable to stop herself just before disconnecting him. She tossed the pictures on the table and went upstairs.

A shower made her feel almost human again and she stood in the doorway to the nursery, reminding herself and the baby that they'd get along fine, just fine without him. She knew it wasn't true, but didn't see any alternative. Forcing herself to do it, she left a brief message on her lawyer's voice mail that she wanted him to make sure her proxy marriage to Mitch wasn't legal or binding.

After that, she went to her bed and tried to sleep. Every time she looked around the room she saw him there. Beside her in the bed, standing in the bathroom doorway a towel slung low on his hips, another blotting moisture from his hair. She saw him with her eyes open and closed. Now she saw him with his arm around a slim blonde woman who wore a bikini to perfection.

She cried it out, hoping tomorrow she'd find the strength to go on without him. Her hand stroked her stomach and the baby kicked at her. Her phone rang several times that night but she let the machine pick up, knowing now wasn't the time to talk to him. She'd already lost her temper once today; she refused to turn into the shrew of a woman she felt herself lapsing into.

Avery had no doubt she could take care of her child, but in the past months the idea of Mitch being a permanent part of their lives had become comforting. The idea jolted her and she remembered she'd been prepared to do this on her own right from the start. Now, she'd revert to her original plans. Technically, nothing they'd done was irreversible at this point. She hadn't put her home up for rent and hadn't burned any bridges in her professional life.

She was thankful she'd restrained from advertising her relationship with Mitch, so that now nobody would press her about her future plans. Let them think what they want, Avery decided. All she knew was that her child wouldn't suffer because of her decisions. Mitch, on the other hand, could just go to hell.

"Great," she said aloud, "Now you're awake!" The kicking settled but didn't stop completely. She drifted into a sleep induced by emotions and bewilderment. For three more days she managed to get by, taking one hour at a time. She hadn't answered Mitch's calls, though there were several messages on the machine each day. Avery had listened to the two he recorded last night, her hand poised to pick up the receiver. But she hadn't. She retreated from him completely and started to figure out how to make her life whole without him.

****

Mitch had spent the last twenty-four hours traveling to get home, and the two days before that trying to get in touch with Avery. He was mad as hell at her and not knowing what set her off was worse. The only thing that mattered was getting home to her. Damn the resort and the grand opening. Deep inside he knew something had triggered her hatred of him. He hadn't heard her use that tone in all the time they'd been together except once, when she'd rounded on him at the hotel in Las Vegas when he finally told her who he really was. He heard the desperation in her voice that time and it made his heart break. He'd find out what button had been pushed and then deal with her. Until then, he had to make due with commercial flights and schedules he couldn't control. He was just a passenger with no say and he hated every hour of it. But once he hit the west coast, his private plane would be waiting.

****

Avery woke in the early morning and knew something was wrong. Although she'd been uncomfortable and moody, she'd been to the doctor just a week before and told everything was on schedule and she'd have her baby in three or four weeks as predicted. But now, only a week later, the moisture between her legs wasn't a good sign. She hesitated, but forced herself to turn on the bedside light, holding back the scream that dashed through her body when she saw red.

She grabbed the phone beside her and called her doctor. After that, it all moved so quickly. The ambulance arrived and took her to the hospital where her doctor was waiting. The rush of strange people around her was frightening. All she could see were the florescent lights above her as they rushed her on a stretcher through the halls. She'd tried to call Mitch, but couldn't reach him. With the time differences and distance, she knew he'd never make it in time to see their baby born. She'd been reassured that the baby was fine and monitors beeped and hissed a steady rhythm in the background as she faded in and out of sleep.

She woke at one point and found Ruth by her bedside, a worried look on her face. "The baby?" she managed to ask in a strangled tone.

"Fine so far," Ruth told her with a smile.

"What's wrong?" Avery never got an answer, the pain took her words. That was all she remembered when she woke. Avery forced herself to swim out of the darkness, forced herself to open her eyes. Her lids fluttered against the overbearing light and she let them close again. It was the warm hand that took hers that forced her to open them once again.

"The baby?"

"You're both fine, going to be fine," Ruth told her, reassuring her.

"What happened?"

"The placenta has started to separate from your

uterine wall…"

"Jr.!" Avery moved her hand to her stomach and still felt the swell beneath it and relaxed back on the pillows. "Mitch. I couldn't get through to Mitch."

"He's on his way; he'll be here as soon as he can. Now, you need to rest a while."

"Ruth, what's wrong? Tell me, please, I need to know."

"They might have to do a cesarean section if…"

Avery burst into tears and didn't care who saw her. "Ruth, promise me, you must make them save the baby, no matter what."

"Don't go there, you'll both be fine."

"Promise me, please?"

"Avery, you're both going to be fine," but the look on her face changed immediately as a monitor beeped a different tone in the background.

Avery tried to sit up and couldn't. There was a rush of people around her again, and all she could do was plead with them to save her baby.

****

The overhead light wasn't glaring; it was horrendous. She knew she was in an operating room and knew she was in good hands, but none of it mattered. Her mind floated in and out of the conversation going on around her but she couldn't understand most of it. She only knew when she heard Mitch's voice bellowing from the hallway that he wouldn't be kept away from his wife and child that their situation had taken a turn for the better. Numb to what was being done to her behind the sheeted partition, she turned to watch him tug on a protective gown, a nurse trotting along behind him trying to tie it in place, before he was at her side.

"Avery, I thought you were going to wait until I got back to have the baby?" he started, but didn't continue when he realized what was happening. His lips went to hers and she started to cry.

"I'm sorry, Mitch, I tried…"

His hand smoothed her forehead and he whispered that everything would be all right. Avery couldn't see his face and wondered if he meant it. He only left her side when the doctor motioned to him. Watching from a hazy cloud, she saw Mitch take something silver and when she blinked, he was standing beside the doctor, a squirming mass in his arms, held tight against his chest.

She struggled to sit forward but a hand held her back. Mitch moved toward her, gently placing the baby on her chest. "Meet our son, Avery," he said, his lips going to her cheek.

She tried to hold him when the nurse swept him away from her, her arms feeling empty already. "We'll clean him up and bring him right back, I promise." Mitch stood by her head, his bloodstained gown still draped over him as he leaned by her. Avery understood the rest of the process of her surgery, but being semi-awake and listening to what was going on and not feeling it was strange. None of it mattered; she just wanted her son back in her arms.

The room was dark when she woke again, the blinds open to the night sky. She tried to move and it all came back to her. The baby, her son, the cesarean section, and Mitch. He'd been beside her, handed her his son for the first time. She allowed the tears to cloud her eyes and turned to find him stretched out in a chair beside her bed. He looked tired and disheveled. Her stirring woke him and he stretched as he woke a smile on his lips.

"How do you feel?" he asked, going to sit on the side of her bed.

"The baby, Mitch?" was all she managed to choke out.

"He's fine, strong and healthy, even if he is three weeks early." He pulled back and studied her face. "Ruth warned you he'd be a handfull," he teased then burst into tears and dragged her to his chest.

She grimaced and he released her, his hands going to her face. “Avery, what happened?”

“I don’t know, the doctor said…”

“No, between us? One day we were fine and the next day you hated me. Why?”

“It doesn’t matter, Mitchell.” She let her body drop back onto the pillows and turned from him. The want to touch him, to comfort him was overwhelming and Avery knew that wouldn’t be her place anymore.

“It does matter, to all three of us!”

Avery heard his words and saw red. She struggled to sit up and started spitting out curse words in Italian at him. Exasperated, she controlled her voice, turning to stare at him. “I’ll not have my son being brought up by your mistress. I’ll fight you so you’d better be prepared. You can see him, but not her!”

“Her who?” Mitch stood and walked to the window, his hand sliding through the top of his dark hair, hair the same color as that on her baby’s head.

“Please don’t pretend. I wish you’d have been honest with me. I’d like to be left alone for a while.” She pressed the call button for the nurse and asked when she could see her baby. Reassured they’d bring him to her, she settled back as best she could and waited, glaring at Mitch the whole time.

****

When the door swung open she expected it to be the nurse. Instead it was Ruth, all smiles, with happiness floating from her every pore. “He’s such a love. How are you feeling Avery?”

Ruth placed a wrapped package on the foot of the bed and put Avery’s small overnight case in the closet. “I brought your things from home. If I forgot anything, I’ll bring it tomorrow. I know it’s late but I wanted to get one more look at my new grandson.” Eyeing the two tense occupants of the room, she pushed on. “Mitch, why on earth would you give

Avery photos of you and Jennifer from five years ago? Quite rude if you ask me," she continued, knowing neither of them was listening.

It didn't matter. She'd broken through the wall they'd built around their hearts in the last days and it was up to them to tear it down. If they could, they might stand a fighting chance to be a real family. And if they didn't, at least it would be due to them, not a vindictive force from the background.

Ruth had taken Mitch's keys and headed back to Avery's to collect her things. She found her suitcase near the front door and walked through to drop the mail and check the answering machine. That was when she'd seen the photos lying on the table. For the life of her she couldn't figure out why Mitch would give Avery these pictures, especially in their current situation.

These last days when Avery receded from her, when Mitch was calling her to find out what happened to make Avery so angry. She'd grabbed the photos and headed back to the hospital, realizing that an outside force was at work.

"Photos of Jennifer?" he asked.

"Five years ago?" Avery asked at the same time.

Ruth burst out laughing and tossed them onto the foot of the bed. Mitch retrieved them and shook his head. "I didn't give them to Avery, Mother, and I don't know who did."

"They were mailed to me earlier this week; the post mark was Sydney."

"They were meant to come between us."

"Why?" Avery struggled to sit forward, her hand stretched toward Mitch. He watched her for only a second before going to her. This time she welcomed his embrace and let him hold her. His warmth, his smell, all overwhelmed her and she began to cry.

"Mitch, I'm sorry," she started, but he hushed her.

"We'll figure it out later, as long as you know

you're my wife, my one and only."

"Mitch, who hates me this much?"

"I'm not sure if it's you or me."

"I figure it was one last grand gesture," Ruth started, reminding them she was still in the room. They both turned to look at her. "Alex is on an extended vacation. Her mother and I spoke last week. She's supposed to be exploring Europe for three months."

"How would she have the photographs?" Avery asked, turning to look at Mitch.

"They were stashed in a desk drawer at my suite in Atlantic City." He started to wonder what else had been removed from the space or gone through and decided to wait until he was there the next time to find out. For now, only Avery mattered, and his son. "I don't know, but I'll find out."

"Let it go, Mitch. If they're from Alex they're a last attempt to come between you two. Don't you think the timing is interesting? The end of Avery's pregnancy, she'd know you were both tense, and she'd know the schedule for the resort opening. She played her last card; don't give her the satisfaction of knowing it even affected you."

"But they did affect us. Avery assumed…"

"Yes, I assumed and I was wrong. Oh, Mitch, I should have asked you." She let her shoulders slump just slightly against his chest, and his hand automatically circled around her.

"I'm going to the nursery for a few minutes," Ruth said, slipping from the room unnoticed so that Mitch and Avery had a moment to themselves.

"I'm sorry; I overreacted, just like I was supposed to." Avery pulled away from him and grabbed the small box of tissues from her bedside table. She handed it to Mitch, who pulled several sheets from the box and wiped his face.

"Why is it I never cried until I met you?" he asked Avery. She stared for only a second then started laughing. "That's better. Avery, are we okay?"

"You tell me. Can you stand to be with me knowing my hormones are raging? I'm short-fused right now."

"If I'd have kept you with me this wouldn't have happened. Even if they'd still been sent, we would have discussed them right away. From now on, if you can't travel with me, I don't go!"

Avery smiled and agreed.

****

They had a short talk with her doctor soon after and learned she was in good shape, all things considered. The baby's weight had most likely caused the separation. They concluded that she had done nothing to trigger it. "Considering he's over ten pounds and twenty-six inches long, that's a belly full for any woman, no matter how big a frame you have," he'd teased. And he told her she shouldn't worry about the next time. Every pregnancy was different and this might never happen again. He left when the nurse brought the baby in, wishing them all well. Mitch straightened the pillows behind her and she struggled to get comfortable. Pulling a second pillow near her side, she took her son from the nurse and brought him to her chest.

"Want some help?" she asked, watching Avery position him at her breast.

"No, thanks, we'd better learn ourselves," she answered. The nurse took her hint and left quietly, closing the door behind her. "Mitch, come here, please."

He moved from the foot of her bed, ready to offer assistance. She took his hand and placed it on his son. Mitch settled beside her, one arm around her shoulders, the other resting on his child. He watched as the baby suckled and said a whispered prayer of thanks.

"You okay?" Avery whispered, "Or is it all too

much?"

"No, I'm better than okay. I'm humbled, Avery. Can you understand that? Here we are, our own family, our son feeding from you. I can't really believe it's all happened."

"Believe it, Mitch. You're stuck with us now."

"Thank you, Avery. For you, for the baby, for what your body went through to give him to us, and for not holding a grudge." His eyebrow rose in a question.

"I jumped to conclusions, Mitch. I should have had more faith in you."

"Yes, but you'll learn with time." He pulled back when she switched the baby to her other breast, then settled beside her once again. "By the way, I told you so," he whispered, his lips to her ear. "Our son..."

She turned to look at him and watched as he unwrapped the baby from his blanket. His large hand and fingers dwarfed the baby as he gently touched each finger and toe. Only when he turned back to her did he smile.

"God, Avery, he's ten pounds of healthy baby boy. Twenty-six inches tall at birth. I think we might have created a basketball player." The baby kicked as if he could understand them.

****

Avery was dressed and ready to go home long before they released her. The two days she'd been forced to stay in the hospital had been hell. All she wanted was to be home with her family. When it finally happened, she'd never felt so at peace. Their first night as a family, she stood beside Mitch staring down at their son in the bassinet beside their bed.

"Don't you think it's time we named him? Baby boy Hamilton isn't going to cut it in kindergarten. Michael M. Hamilton, the third?" Avery asked.

"No Mickey, though," Mitch said. "I want a stronger nickname for our son."

"How about Trey?"

"I could get used to that," he said.

Avery leaned down and ran her finger along the baby's cheek. "What about you, big guy, do you like Trey?" The small face below them seemed to smile and they knew his fate was sealed. Michael Mitchell Hamilton the third, Trey Hamilton, had come home.

Sitting propped in their master bed, Avery nursed her son while Mitch looked on.

Moving behind her, he slipped a necklace around her throat and clasped it in place. Her hand moved to it, taking it from her skin to look at it. The center stone swung freely on the chain, a diamond that matched the center stone of her engagement ring.

"Mitch?"

"It was a matched set," he told her as he kissed her. "A gift from your son."

"And his father?"

"And your husband."

"We never did get around to taking care of that. Is my son legal or not?"

"He's ours and that makes him wonderful, no matter what our marital status is."

"That's a fine diversion, Mitch, but really, which is it?"

Epilogue

Mitch put a glass of wine on the table in front of Avery. She nodded her thanks but didn't touch it. Trey played with his toy trucks a few feet away on the sand, his dark brown hair and eyes resembled Mitch's baby pictures. His younger sister sat beside him, awkwardly dumping small shovelfuls of sand into the plastic bucket in front of her. Her lighter eyes and reddish hair told anyone who saw her she was Avery's daughter. Mitch had been lying beside her, teaching her the finer art of building a sand castle, just before he brought her the wine.

"What's wrong, Avery? You haven't touched your wine and you've got that faraway look in your eye." He moved his chair closer beside her, watching her play with the chain that now held two identical diamonds. He took the chain from her fingers and stared at it.

"Nothing's wrong, except, Mitch, we have to push back the wedding for a while."

It seemed to Avery that just when she felt she was getting some semblance of her old body back, she got pregnant. Now she'd lose the small indents at her waist. How many sit ups had she done to earn them? On a second breath, the idea that she and Mitch had created a new life thrilled her beyond any smaller dress size.

Mitch was involved with the children and with her, seemingly enjoying the time he experienced with her while she carried Sara. We're going to need our sense of humor this time around, thinking of Trey and his activity level as well as Sara's. Feeling lighter in mind and spirit if not body, the corners of her mouth tilted into a strange smile.

"No, Avery. That's what you told me when Trey was two. Then we had Sara and you told me we had to wait. We're going to have our wedding this time."

"We can't. How can we be married when this one is born when we weren't for the other two?" She watched him finally understand her meaning.

"This your way of telling me it's time to get another stone for your necklace?"

"Yes. Do you have a problem with that?"

"Only that we'll have to wait to get married. We wouldn't want to traumatize Trey or Sara would we?" He moved closer to her, "I'm very happy, Avery. Thank you." His kiss told her his words were true. "The lodge?" he asked, taking a sip from his glass just before he dropped his finger into the liquid and ran it over her lips, his tongue following closely behind.

"Yes, the lodge," she said, a little too breathless for both their comforts. He stood quickly and moved towards the house.

"Mom, are you busy?" he yelled and waited until she walked onto the patio.

"Just reading. What's going on?"

"We're going for a walk; can you keep an eye on the kid's until Margie gets back from town?"

"Of course," she told him on her way toward the sand box, dropping easily onto the small wooden bench side. Mitch grabbed Avery's hand and walked her toward the vineyard.

"How long have you known?" he asked, his arm protectively around her shoulder.

"This morning I did a home test. Are you okay with this, Mitch? I seem to get pregnant if you kiss me."

"It took a lot more than a kiss to get you pregnant, Mrs. Hamilton."

He reached the small grassy clearing he'd headed for and dropped to his knees. "Come and relax; I'll refresh your memory."

And he did, in all the wonderful ways he touched and loved her. Their joining hadn't been fast and furious as it was at times, but it had been powerful and erotic. He was buttoning his shirt when he reached down his hand to help her up.

"And that, Mrs. Hamilton, is how you keep getting pregnant."

"Now I understand, but I have a few questions," she whispered, her hand going to cover his maleness. Even through his denim jeans she could feel his arousal. Throwing back her head and laughing, she moved to take his mouth under hers. It was the second time they were getting dressed that he smiled at her.

"We'll push the wedding off, Avery. You're my wife, anyway; you always have been."

"But you said the proxy was just a joke that..." He gave her his, "we'll talk about it later" smile and turned away. "Michael Mitchell Hamilton, am I married to you or not? Because if I am, the lawyer is gonna have a field day with you..."

Her words changed into Italian and he started to laugh. His kiss cut off her tirade of words and took the fight out of her.

"Always my wife and the mother of my children, as many as you'll give me, Avery."

"Yes, Mitch, always yours."

A kiss sealed their fate.

Thank you for purchasing this Wild Rose Press publication. For other wonderful stories of romance, please visit our on-line bookstore at www.thewildrosepress.com.

For questions or more information contact us at info@thewildrosepress.com.

The Wild Rose Press
www.TheWildRosePress.com

www.ingramcontent.com/pod-product-compliance
Lightning Source LLC
LaVergne TN
LVHW050644100826
845148LV00011B/1969

* 9 7 8 1 6 0 1 5 4 5 3 8 1 *